DEATH, FAMILY, AND LOVE

DEATH, FAMILY, AND LOVE

Michael H. Mitias

RESOURCE *Publications* • Eugene, Oregon

DEATH, FAMILY, AND LOVE

Resource Publications
An Imprint of Wipf and Stock Publishers
199 W. 8th Ave., Suite 3
Eugene, OR 97401

www.wipfandstock.com

PAPERBACK ISBN: 978-1-7252-8049-6
HARDCOVER ISBN: 978-1-7252-8050-2
EBOOK ISBN: 978-1-7252-8051-9

Contents

CHAPTER ONE

Dr. Athenaion Meets the God of Death

Dr. Anat Athenaion was absorbed in a meditation on Hegel's conception of the good society when she heard three soft knocks at the door of her apartment. She was startled, and to some extent annoyed, because she was not expecting any visitors, not on a Sunday morning, and because she was in the heat of a creative act. She was about to articulate a new interpretation of the much-discussed and spectacularly misunderstood concept of "ethical society." That is, of a society in which people can flourish as *human individuals*, one that is vitally relevant to a society that seems to be increasingly dominated and governed by political, economic, religious, and scientific technocrats. She felt that this on-going development would inevitably undermine the essential conditions of human growth and development: freedom, justice, compassion, creativity, and friendship. If you deprive people of these qualities, you necessarily reduce them to social, economic, or political robots. You deprive them of the capacity to be *human individuals*, that is, the capacity to be self-determined human beings, beings who can chart the course of their lives and assume responsibility for it.

People who cannot assume this kind of responsibility are like sheep led by a shepherd, not like shepherds who lead their lives. But Dr. Athenaion believed that human beings are created to be, or become, human individuals. She never tired of asking her students, "Do you want to be a sheep or the master of your life? Do you want to be fattened and then led to the slaughterhouse without knowing why? Do you want someone to control your life?" She never tired of challenging them to think, feel, and make life-changing decisions using their minds and wills. She always reminded her students that humanity and, consequently, human individuality, is given to us as a potentiality awaiting realization and that we are responsible for realizing it. Human individuality, she once argued, is not only the most fundamental human right but also our *destiny*: "Yes, becoming who we are as human beings is our destiny in this world! Do you want someone to fashion your destiny?"

"The point," she argued one day in her Existentialism class, "is not merely to think, feel, and act is not merely to be alive or to know how to survive. The animals in the wild are quite proficient in the art of survival. The point is to think, feel, and live *as a human being*. Be true to yourself! Take charge of your destiny! Live from the human spark that sits at the base of your heart. This spark is a divine gift. It is a cry for being. Be a cry for being! Be a living light of this spark!"

"Please remember that you are not granted this gift as a readymade reality but as a possibility, as a promise, as a potentiality awaiting realization by you and no one else. You are born as a human individual in the process of realizing it. Do not look for your destiny in some distant future, in the hands of philosophers, priests, legislators, scientists, society, or chance. Look for it in this spark, in this shining jewel of humanity. The materials and the elements for designing and building your true self, therefore, of your destiny, are hidden inside it. Only when you stand on your feet and fashion its structure with your hands can you thrive as a human being. Only then can you be an actor on the stage of human life, and only then can you justify the life you have lived. Otherwise, you will remain a spectator, and you will die without knowing what your life was about."

Dr. Athenaion paused for a few moments, gazing thoughtfully into the corner on the right of the lecture room, and with a *mystical posture of mind*, she continued, "Yes, only when you participate in the rite of human life as an actor can you move closer to God as your ultimate object of love and desire. Only then can you be a part of the creative spirit, the *geist*, that energizes the course of human civilization. Only then can you feel the pulse of life that radiates from this spirt and relish the joy it produces in your heart. And yes, only then can you think, feel, and know what it means *to be*. You are created to be, but you cannot be until you feel this joy in your heart. It may seem strange, at least to some of you, that only when you feel the presence of God can you become part of the creative spirit that underlies the cosmic process. Only then can you love God directly, and only then can you glorify him truly: How can you glorify him if you do not feel his presence if you do not feel his radiance? Has it occurred to you that the strongest urge of this divine spark is to partake in the cosmic process? Has it occurred to you that being such a participant is the ultimate source of inspiration in designing and implementing our life-projects?"

"Tell me, have you participated in the rite of creation in any sphere of human experience—art, science, philosophy, religion, politics, or your personal life? Have you felt the thrill of this type of activity—creative activity? Now, focus your attention not on mundane activities that you frequently perform during your ordinary life, but on the activity of creating yourself, which is the unfolding of your destiny in every moment of your existence. This activity is the source of the joy your heart craves more than anything in the world. Its domain is not your library, your ivory tower, your office, your garden, or any other type of mental or physical space but your social existence in which you meet your *basic needs as a human being*, namely your aesthetic, religious, intellectual, professional, and cultural needs. The process of meeting these needs is the medium in which you transform the divine spark in your heart into the human individual you should be. You exist, and you shine as a self in what you do, or rather in what you create. Your deeds, regardless of whether they are theoretical, practical, professional, or artistic, are the building blocks of the frame of your character. The promotion of good should form the foundation from which your actions radiate. Your self is true since your actions originate from your goodwill. Some actions are constructive, and some are destructive; some are morally good, and some are morally bad; some are admirable, and some are despicable. The building blocks of the true self are good actions primarily because the good is constructive, and the bad is destructive. You cannot dismiss what I have just said as fancy, abstract, or idle talk unless you first know what you are dismissing, and you cannot know what you are dismissing unless you feel the radiance of the cosmic spirit that pulsates not only in the cosmic process but also in the spark that shines like a sun in your heart. Otherwise, like those sheep, you will live and die without knowing why you lived and died. Besides, what if what you are dismissing is really gold and not straw?"

"Don't let those teachers, priests, sophists, parents, and social charlatans, or the "they," the invisible, inaudible "they" around you, persuade you that you exist to seek pleasure, accumulate wealth, power, life, social glory, or knowledge, for these authorities live on the fringe of the cosmic process, not as participants in its creative vision and power. No, you exist to be a creator, to promote goodness in your life and the lives of others, but how can you create goodness if you are not a human individual? And how can you be a human individual if you do not create yourself since you are given to the world as a potentiality for becoming a human individual?"

These rhetorical questions flowed from Dr. Athenaion's mouth the way flames of fire flow from a crackling hearth. A philosophical angel would say that *she was on fire*. She paused for a few seconds, caught her breath, and then continued, "The point is not to seek happiness as a goal existing somewhere in your mind, in the future, or even in heaven, because it is not and cannot be a goal. It is not a clearly defined concept or ideal. No two human beings, philosophers, scientists, or theologians, have agreed on its nature, existence, or even desirability. But suppose it is or can be a goal, then where, when, and under what conditions can it be attained by any particular individual who lives in a certain place and historical epoch? Can you say that you are happy when you are young, in the middle of your life, or at its end? Does it signify some type of reward we receive when we retire after forty years of work? But what is the use of such a reward if we have already reached the end of our lives?"

"If happiness is a meaningful goal, it should permeate and energize every action we perform in our lives. We should be able to feel it amid adversities. You should not confuse *happiness* with *pleasure*. The first is a permanent possession, the second is a temporary feeling; the first is an achievement, the second is produced by physical or psychological influence; the first is indifferent to pain, the second shies away from pain; the first aims at the good in itself, the second aims at the good of the individual. But the more important fact you should remember is that happiness cannot be provided by any person, organization, or agency, regardless of the nature of its power; it is a personal achievement. You may give me pastries, knowledge, food, smiles, shelter, or a job, and you may create the conditions for me to be successful, but you cannot give me happiness. Moreover, happiness is not a special kind of experience in any particular circumstance, and we cannot be happy at a preconceived time like now, a little later, today, tomorrow, or sometime in the future. A happy person is always happy. It is challenging to identify happiness as it relates to a specific experience."

"*Happiness is a spiritual state or orientation*. It emerges from the way our lives are lived, and the way of life that leads to the emergence of this spiritual state is a good life, the kind of life that is founded in the values of truth, beauty, and goodness, such as justice, friendship, honesty, courage, serving others, compassion, mercy, grandeur, wisdom, and grace, to mention just a few values. Happy people do not know that they are happy: *they are happy*. They know that they should pursue the good, the beautiful, and the true in their daily lives, regardless of whether it is in the sphere of work, family, school, government, or any other domain! Does the scientist in their laboratory, the artist in their studio, the social reformer among the poor, the sick, the disenfranchised, and the oppressed, the archaeologist at a historical site, the teacher in the classroom, or the farmer in the field—yes, do these and millions of other people worry, or even think, of their happiness when they are in the midst of their work? Happy people are *service-minded people*, not *happiness-minded people*. They feel good, have inner peace, and experience a sense of fulfillment when they accomplish an important task, one that promotes the good of society, a particular person, or a group of persons."

"As a spiritual state, happiness is a *gift of goodness*. This gift is not a reward but a natural emanation of good action. However, it is not an ordinary emanation, mainly because by its very essence, it is a living flame, a thrust of life, of light, the kind that illuminates the meaning of being and especially humanity. I liken the human being to a tree that produces life-enhancing fruits. Doesn't the artist experience a deep feeling of satisfaction, of delight, of pride, of inner growth, in short, of joy, when they stand before a painting they have just completed successfully? Don't they frown upon the anxiety, the fears, the frustration, the pain they experienced while working on it? What is pain to joy, to the feeling of inner growth—of being, of being-in-growth? Suppose we ask the artist—" But Dr. Athenaion could not complete her sentence because the bell rang. Although she stopped the lecture, the students did not leave their chairs. Their eyes lingered on the face of their professor as if to say, "Continue!"

"We shall continue this discussion next Monday," Dr. Athenaion said in a subdued voice, "but not now because the Dean recently instructed the faculty to stop their lectures at the end of the hour. He does not want students to be late for their subsequent classes. I wish you a pleasant and productive weekend."

The purpose of the preceding excerpt from Dr. Athenaion's lecture, dear reader, was simply to give you an idea about the kind of person and thinker she was, and the reason that prompted those three soft knocks at the door of her apartment that Sunday morning!

As I mentioned earlier, Dr. Athenaion was in the heat of a creative act when those three knocks disrupted a meditation she was having on Hegel's conception of "ethical society" and the extent to which this conception can form the basis for an effective and practical social reform program under which a society governed by technocrats can thrive as *a community of human individuals.* Dr. Athenaion was stranded between two equally strong obligations when those knocks disrupted the thread of her meditation: the obligation to pursue her meditation on the possibility of a human society governed by technocrats, which is a supremely valuable undertaking, and the obligation to respond to the caller who might be a student or a neighbor in need of urgent assistance, which is also supremely valuable. It took her a few seconds to extricate herself from the conflict created by these two obligations only because the knocks persisted, culminating in three more knocks. She decided to respond to the caller. She argued that she could reflect again on the Hegelian conception of an ethical society, but she could not repair the harm she might cause to a needy friend, student, or person if she declined to open the door.

Without hesitation, Dr. Athenaion placed her pen on the desk and sprinted to her bedroom. She stopped for a moment before the mirror of her dresser. She eyed her disheveled hair and promptly rolled it into a knot at the back of her head. She pulled a long robe over her short pajamas, smoothed her rumpled eyebrows, and dashed to the door. She peered through the peephole to ascertain the identity of the caller. A young man was standing on the other side of the door. He was neither a neighbor nor one of her students. Nevertheless, she opened the door without faltering only because she always acted from an innocent heart and mind and because the caller might be one of her older students.

A strikingly handsome young man greeted Dr. Athenaion's eyes when she opened the door. He was slim and tall with hazel eyes beneath thick eyebrows. His upper lip was graced with a neatly trimmed mustache, while his head was covered with a panoply of black hair. He was dressed in a white sweater, light brown trousers, and brown shoes. Although he was a flame of youth, it was difficult to estimate his age. But one could conjecture that he was in his mid-thirties. It seemed to Dr. Athenaion that he was a kind of Don Juan. She was about to smile because she never expected to meet such a character in her life. And yet, such a character was standing before her on her doorstep as a real human being. Her immediate impulse was to examine his complexion and bodily gestures because she was curious to know the kind of character he was. Yet, to her disappointment, he did not reveal any kind of character trait, physical or mental. He struck her more as a figure who has just stepped out of a painting created by Norma Rockwell than a person who typically walks the streets of social life.

Dr. Athenaion was a kind, genial, and generous woman. She ordinarily welcomed her visitors into her apartment spontaneously without questioning their intensions or asking about the purpose of their visit, but that morning, and for a mysterious reason she could not decipher, she could not welcome the exceedingly good-looking man into her apartment. She felt an urgent desire to know his identity and the purpose of his call first. But unfortunately, both his identity and the purpose of his call were hidden behind his elegant appearance. Her ignorance of his identity, especially the fact that she had never seen a Don Juan on the campus of Union College or anywhere in Jackson, intensified her curiosity and created a feeling of awkwardness in her mind. She hesitated; she could neither dismiss him, for she had no justifiable reason to do so nor welcome him, for she could not admit a person into her apartment without knowing their identity or intentions. The caller noticed her awkwardness and felt her hesitation. His blank, almost impassive expression, which was a factor in instigating her reluctance, suddenly changed into a pleasant countenance. It seemed as if his face, which was beautiful by any measure of beauty, was abruptly aglow with an effusion of a special kind of radiance. A seductive smile surged from the midst of that radiance, and in a friendly voice, he said, "Dr. Athenaion, you are well known for your hospitality and especially for your generous heart. There is no reason for denying me the honor of a short visit with the most distinguished teacher, scholar, social servant, and one of the finest citizens of the city of Jackson." Astonished, and for a moment speechless, she looked at the caller and focused her critical attention on his countenance, the same countenance that was blank and impassive a few seconds earlier. A rather strange, inscrutable feeling rose in her mind. The sudden transformation she just witnessed defied logical and conceptual comprehension. Frankly, it was unbelievable. She sank into a moment of thoughtfulness, of bafflement, of fear! The feeling of hesitation that crept into her mind as a normal mental state earlier now became a feeling of existential confusion, one that verged on anxiety. She did not respond to the caller's complimentary remark. She could not! How could she? What kind of response could she have delivered? To whom should she respond—to the impassive, soul-less Don Juan or to the warm, alluring Don Juan? Which one of the two was the real visitor? How could this sudden, instantaneous transformation of personality, of demeanor, take place? How would you, dear reader, act in such a situation? But Dr. Athenaion was a philosopher; she was a keen analyst, not only of ideas but also of human character and human circumstances. She was always disinclined to act hastily or irrationally. But the situation she was in that morning defied logical analysis, much less understanding. She did not respond to the caller, not immediately; she looked at him inquisitively yet critically. The only feeling, not even an idea that crawled into her consciousnesses, was to dismiss him politely and close the door in his face, albeit softly. She couldn't be part of a vague, irrational, and possibly dangerous encounter. No human being would fault her had she made this decision. But the caller, who knew Dr. Athenaion quite well, to the extent that he was reading her mind throughout this conversation, understood the strangeness as well as the complexity of the situation he had created for her. "There is no need to fear me, Dr. Athenaion," he suddenly said, "or to worry about your physical or mental wellbeing, fame, power, or profession. I only wish to have a conversation with you. Is this too much to ask?"

"But, first, who are you?" Dr. Athenaion asked, a tinge of seriousness and self-confidence in her voice. "I do not know you! I have the absolute right to know the people I converse with." Dr. Athenaion did not believe in the existence of non-natural and non-human spirits or spirit-like beings, and yet, what she had witnessed was neither natural nor human. "There are many types of visits. Some are meaningful and some frivolous," she reasoned. "I am not interested in frivolous ones, they are a waste of time. How can I have a conversation with a person I do not know?" Besides, there was something mysterious, uncanny about him. He was real and unreal, honest and deceptive, human, and un-human at the same time. She surveyed his face again mainly to ascertain whether the man standing at the threshold of her door was a real human being. Again, she hesitated in arriving at a decision.

"I would be happy to tell you who I am, and I would be equally happy to inform you of the purpose of my visit. As far as I know, you've never conducted any of your visits or any of your serious conversations at the threshold of your door. I shall be honored if you welcome me into your home the way you welcome all your visitors." The caller made this request with a friendly, and an objective observer would say alluring, smile. But Dr. Athenaion did not observe this aspect of his request because she was trying to make sense of the caller's presence at the door of her apartment.

"*As far as you know*? You seem to presume much, much more than you should," Dr. Athenaion snapped involuntarily.

"Yes, like other people, people you have not taught and people you have not met personally, know about you. You are a very renowned person, Dr. Athenaion," The caller emphasized. "You are a highly respected and admired model of a human being."

"I am not fishing for a compliment."

"Of that, I am certain. I just wanted to assure you of my serious intentions and the fact that your reputation precedes you everywhere you go."

Although reluctantly and with a streak of fear in her mind, Dr. Athenaion admitted the caller into her apartment. The living room was adjacent to her study. Before moving to the sofa, where he was expected to sit, her guest stopped at the door of the study and scanned it with curious eyes. "This is where Dr. Athenaion gives birth to her philosophical vision of a human community governed by technocrats, and this is where she converses with the great minds in the history of philosophy." He nodded, contracted his eyes, and cast a sharp look at a lithograph hanging over a large bookcase. "Hegel, ha?"

"Yes."

"You admire him?"

"He is a very insightful philosopher. His work is a rich source of ideas and possibilities of new ways of theorizing about the nature of the world and human life."

"People like him are dangerous."

"Dangerous?" Dr. Athenaion frowned with a palpable feeling of dissatisfaction. "On the contrary, he is one of the most constructive philosophers of all time. His philosophy is the source of most, if not all, the metaphysical and social schools of thought in the nineteenth and twentieth centuries."

"What you say is a matter of opinion," the visitor mumbled as he walked toward the sofa. "How is your work on the project of the development of a human community governed by technocrats going?" The visitor asked as he sat on the right corner of the sofa.

Dr. Athenaion was about to sit in a chair facing her visitor when this question pierced her ears like an arrow of fire. She remained standing and stared at him, anger in her eyes, and a severe frown on her forehead. "He seems to know a great deal about my social standing, which is public knowledge, but about my project and about what I am thinking and how I am feeling?" she thought. "This is impossible! Has he been spying on me?

Has he been breaking into my apartment during my absence when I am at the college and during the night when I am asleep? Has he been prying into my documents, papers, and letters? How did he know that I was meditating on Hegel's conception of the ethical state and that I am investigating the possibility of a human community governed by technocrats? What is his purpose? What does he expect from me?" She trembled and clenched her teeth hard to stop her lower jaw from shaking. She could neither think nor feel because she did not know what to believe and how to feel. Her mind was in a state of turmoil. She looked at him again and frowned. "Is this Don Juan real? Am I standing before a phantasmagoria?" These questions coursed through her mind rapidly and did not linger only because her guest threw a calm, cold-blooded glance her way. "Why don't you sit, Dr. Athenaion?" he said, "I would very much enjoy a conversation with you on the nature and viability of a human community governed by technocrats. I doubt that any philosopher at Union or any other institution of higher learning is as conversant on this subject as you." But Dr. Athenaion was not interested in any kind of conversation at that moment, at least not with that creature.

With her eyes still fixed on him and with her frown still looming on her forehead, Dr. Athenaion asked again, "*Who are you*?"

"If my identity is more important to you than a meaningful conversation on a concept you consider vitally important, I shall be happy to oblige you," the visitor said in the same calm, cold-blooded manner. Unaware of what she was doing, Dr. Athenaion slowly, very slowly, slid into her armchair without lifting her angry eyes from his face.

"Yes, I would like to be obliged," she said after she sat in her chair.

"I am Mowt, *the God of Death*!"

Mowt was the God of Death in Ugarit, a kingdom that flourished on the eastern coast of the Mediterranean during the second and first millennia, B.C. He is and always was a mythical deity. Dr. Athenaion was aware of this fact. However, the claim that the man sitting on the sofa opposite her was Mowt did not irritate her because she knew that she was not sitting in the presence of a god. What annoyed her and robbed her peace of mind was the way he behaved, and he did not act like a normal human being. Indeed, nothing about him, not even his appearance, was normal. Did she admit an anomaly to her apartment? Was she talking to a rare mutant? She could not dwell on these questions because her guest was waiting for an answer to his question and because she was anxious to discover his true identity.

"You can borrow the name of any god, any emperor, any genius, any saint, even the name of the devil. This does not matter to me."

"Are you sure?" The guest interrupted her. "Have you forgotten that famous question, what is in a name?"

"A name is only a name, no more than a name. Do not give your imagination unnecessary wings!"

"Is the name a name if it does not name a particular object? How does it point to what it names? What do you think when someone utters the name 'Plato'?"

"What is Plato but his deeds or achievements? What if an idiot calls himself Plato, here I mean the man who flourished in Athens twenty-four hundred years ago, wouldn't you chuckle? A fool can call himself Plato, but he remains a fool. What 'Plato' means and what 'fool' means are different from each other. 'Plato' denotes a particular person. I am interested in the identity of the man who calls himself 'Mowt': the God of Death."

"You deserve the respect accorded you by your students and colleagues."

"I am not interested in what you or others think of me, I am interested in an answer to my question."

"I am not the mythical Mowt; I am the real Mowt, the God of Death! I am the power that supervises *human* affairs and determines their *human death*. I am the living embodiment of this power. To be clear, I am the real embodiment of the god of *human death*! And, let me rush to add that I am as real as everything in this world is real. Neither you nor any other human being can afford to ignore, deny, or in any way underestimate my powers."

"Let me remind you that we do not live in the dark ages. We live in the age of reason, of technology, of the highest promise of human nature. Any discourse on supernatural or superhuman beings is meaningless. Mythical deities, places, and empires are fictions that exist in the minds of some human beings." The guest was grinding his teeth, his lips were pursed, and his eyes were spouting sparks of anger.

"Am I a fiction? Are you conversing with a fiction? Is a fiction sitting on the sofa in your living room?"

"I am talking with a human being. You are not a fiction; therefore, you are not the living reality of Mowt."

"Have you heard of the ego-centric predicament, Dr. Athenaion?"

"You should take the *Introduction to Logic* course at Union College."

"This is my very point. You are a prisoner to one kind of logic, your logic, the logic you teach, the same logic that governs your way of thinking.

You think that it is the only measure of truth and falsehood, reality and unreality, good and evil because its rules are conducive to the survival of the human race in this kind of natural environment—Earth. But, what if the conditions of human survival change? Wouldn't you need another logic to survive under the new conditions of life? What if there are rational beings who surpass your capacities of thinking, feeling, and willing. Have you, as an instantiation of humanity, installed yourself as the god who created you and the universe? What you call logic is the product of the natural process—of the struggle of the human species to survive over millions of years. But you should remember that my existence and my function in your world are not governed by human laws but by the law of The One. Have you ever tried to lift your mind, when you meditated on the cause and nature of the universe, to the logic of the power that created this whole cosmic spectacle?

"I have, but what you say does not make sense."

"Do you mean that what I say does not agree with, or fit, your capacity of logical comprehension? Can you agree, or disagree, with me on anything except according to the capacity of your comprehension, which confirms the validity of my claim that you are a prisoner to your logical faculty and that the eyes of your mind cannot see the possibility of other equally valid ways of thinking?"

"You seem to have studied some philosophy, but unfortunately, you are more of a sophist than a philosopher."

"Let me assure you that I am neither a philosopher nor a sophist. Do you think I am foolish enough to live in the prison of your logical way of thinking or to restrict my existence to your puny world? Matters of existence and non-existence cannot be decided or understood by your logic. The only class of objects, whose existence and non-existence can be decided or understood by your logic is the class you call artifacts. Every other type of existence and non-existence are decided and understood according to laws that surpass your capacity of understanding. The laws that govern my existence and functions transcend the capacity of your understanding. These laws emanate directly from The One. Have you ever thought, or even dared to think, of standing on The Edge, the very edge of the universe? Have you ever tried to probe the mystery of the infinity of the infinite Dark, that stretches before your minuscule mind? If you venture into this type of experience, you will see a glimmer of the light that emanates from it. Anyone who embarks on this adventure would mock your logic and would certainly put your metaphysical speculations in the wastebasket that sits at the side of your desk. Be assured, Dr. Athenaion, that I am real and, more importantly, I am the master of human death."

"I cannot waste my time on your sophistry and meaningless claims." Dr. Athenaion said and was about to ask her uninvited guest to leave her apartment. But she could not declare her wish because he was neither ready nor willing to withdraw from her presence.

"If not on sophistry, on what subject do you wish to spend your time? Has it occurred to you that most of the books, articles, and documentaries on philosophy that fill the libraries and bookstores of the world, not to mention private libraries, are nothing more than sophistry presented as serious philosophy? Haven't you noticed that even the so-called serious philosophers are not interested in wisdom and the good life, that is, in truth, goodness, and beauty? How many of them regularly demonstrated in the streets against the atrocities committed by the Nazi, the Soviet, and the Fascist states during and after the Second World War? How many of them now march in the streets at least once a week against corruption in the main social institutions, including schools and churches? How many of them speak against the neglect of the poor, the disenfranchised, the illiterate, and the oppressed? How many of them speak out against the violence inflicted on the innocent at home, in the office, and the classrooms, even in the church? No, Dr. Athenaion, your philosophers are not interested in the ideals of wisdom, and they are not interested in the betterment of human society. They do not give a hoot about these ideals. They are interested in survival—in their security, pleasure, fame, and fake immortality. Remove the robe of philosophy they wear in the classroom or the marketplace and observe how they actually think, feel, desire, and what they expect from themselves and life in general. In short, observe them stripped of their social and academic dress, and you will see mediocrity staring you in the face. You will see selfish, fickle, frightened human beings who sell empty ideas in the name of truth. You will see the same priests who abandoned their flocks the moment their survival was threatened when the Bubonic plague struck Europe during the fourteenth century. The majority of your philosophes are businesspeople. The difference between them and the professional businesspeople found in commerce, industry, and the ordinary marketplace is that most of the contemporary philosophers pretend to be devotees of the truth the way the priests of the Middle Ages pretended to be the disciples of Christ! They act as philosophers in the classroom, when they write books or articles, and when they read papers at academic conferences and symposia.

The ideas they communicate to their students or colleagues are commodities. These concepts do not originate from their minds and hearts. But we can discuss this subject in detail later, not now."

"What analogy! What presumption! You speak as if you have witnessed and examined the different philosophical communities during the past twenty-seven hundred years, as if you have visited their souls, minds, and hearts."

"It is not a question of 'as if' but of 'act.' Yes, I've witnessed and examined them in the privacy of their souls, minds, and hearts—and yours, too, Dr. Athenaion! You are a rare exception. You are a living flame of the philosophical spirit. I am not interested in dead minds—regardless of whether they dwell in the area of science, religion, politics, or art. I am interested in genuine, creative, visionary human beings. This is why I am here in your apartment this morning! Trust me!"

"Trust me!" Dr. Athenaion repeated with a distinct feeling of irritation. "Trust *is earned*. Nothing you said and did so far inspires trust. Who are you? What is the purpose of your *intrusion*?"

"Is it fair to call a visit you voluntarily allowed an intrusion?"

"Yes, *now* I can call it an intrusion."

"Why?"

"Because your claim that you are the God of Death is preposterous, indeed insulting me. Besides, your intrusion is harmful to me. A frivolous visit is not a visit, but a waste of time. Such a visit is an intrusion."

"Harmful? How?"

"You have pulled me out of productive meditation, you have stolen valuable time from me, and now, contrary to any norm of courtesy, you are forcing me to indulge in a meaningless conversation. Moreover, how did you know the subject of my meditation?"

"I shall answer your question if you promise to be open-minded and willing to entertain ideas that transcend the rules of your logic."

"I am always open-minded and shall think reflectively and critically on what you say. But I shall analyze what you say according to the rules of human logic because they are the only basis for determining the truth or falsity or senselessness of any judgment or point of view."

"You are generous and tolerant. First, I am not a spy, and I am not a prowler. Be assured that I shall not, in any way, violate the integrity of your mind or body."

"But then," Dr. Athenaion intervened, "how did you know the theme of my meditation?"

"Here comes the rub!"

"What do you mean?"

"I am a god, and as a god, I can assume the form of any human being, animal, plant, and physical or non-physical being. I can be here, there, or anywhere at the speed of light and even faster than the speed of light. I can see through the inner essence of things, mental or physical, without penetrating their doors or windows, or walls, and yet remain the god I am."

"This is impossible. Even the gods of antiquity did not undergo a transformation of identity. They were created to perform certain functions, and they could not infringe on the functions of other gods."

"I do not infringe on the function of other gods. My function is to administer the human death of particular people."

"What people?"

"Genuine intellectuals and those who are truly committed to the advancement of human ideals and especially to their implementation. Any intellectual who plays a constructive role in the development of human culture is a project of the God of Love, my uncle's adversary. I am my uncle's assistant. My task is to see to it that the projects of this class of people are aborted before they see the light of day. But I cannot perform my function adequately unless I can undergo a transformation of identity. Anyway, why should you be surprised if you encounter a god who possesses this capacity? As a philosopher, you have all the intellectual and physical powers that enable you to survive. Similarly, as the God of Death, I was created with the capacity to assume any identity I need to perform my function. My uncle is a very busy deity. He frequently asks me to administer the death of die-hard intellectuals. I was able, after a long apprenticeship, to refine the skill of managing the death of such intellectual."

"What are your skills?"

"I am a corrupter, and my means of corruption is seduction."

"Seduction?" Dr. Athenaion asked.

"Yes, it is the most powerful method I use to achieve my purpose. There are many types of seduction: pleasure, power, sex, beauty, wealth, knowledge, romance, social glory, success. In short, anything the human heart desires. The means of seduction I employ are always tailored to the needs and intellectual and moral refinement of my clients. I am willing and ready to corrupt any individual by the most effective means of seduction appropriate to the individual. My ultimate aim is to undermine any decision, action, project, or any ideal or work of the God of Love. The God of Love is a god of construction. My uncle, the god of hate, is the God of Perishing. I delight in destruction. I oversee the death of the *humanity of the individua*l, while my uncle oversees their *physical perishing*."

"Do you really think," Dr. Athenaion asked provocatively, "that hate is more powerful than love?"

"Of course!" Mowt replied with a sarcastic, arrogant chuckle.

"Are you sure?"

"Certainly!"

"What makes you sure?"

"I can refer you to the long list of my achievements if you wish, but since you are a philosopher, I shall speak your language. First, it is impossible for the idea of love to exist without the idea of hate, or the idea of construction to exist without the idea of destruction. The idea of love logically implies the idea of hate. In a state of 'all love,' any action, motive, goal, thought, or feeling we experience cannot be qualified as either hate or love, and in a state of 'all hate,' nothing in this state can be qualified as hate or love. In a state of 'all love' hate or destruction would not exist. People would not possess the consciousness of hate or destruction. But such a state never existed and will never exist. Hate has always existed side by side with love. We know the meaning of love as love only because we know, and experience hate and destruction. Therefore, we know what it means for something to signify construction only because we know what it means for something to denote destruction. But love is not only an idea; it is a fact, and it is a fact merely because hate is a fact. Only those who know the true meaning of love, those who Iive it and are devoted to it, know the true meaning of hate. It may strike you as strange if I say that the seeds of destruction are planted in the core of every human being, every plant, every animal, in short, everything that exists, so that the moment it comes into being it begins to pass out of being. Observe the events of nature and the action of human beings as cosmic occasions. Can you, or anyone, overlook the prevalence of destruction in the natural and human worlds?

"Now, focus your investigative attention on the destructive power of hate. Can you deny it is greater than the power of love? Have you noticed that the books of the philosophers, social scientists, and theologians revolve around love, and how the sermons of the priests, the lectures of the philosophers, and the manifestoes of the social reformers, even of some politicians, fill the air with the word 'love'? But as an honest and accomplished philosopher, have you noticed how the distinguished leaders of your culture manage to appear as disciples of the God of Love while, in fact, they are mediocre, selfish human beings? Love has become a commodity for sale by these leaders. They and most of the people around you wear this love dress in public because it is advantageous and because this is the 'proper' way to appear in society. Do they wear it in the privacy of their homes, of their souls? Social workers have long lists of children, wives, handicapped, and old people who are battered at home. Pedophiles run rife in various churches and organizations. Women and children are sexually harassed in schools. Minorities and poor people in the different segments of society are discriminated against, while the degradation of secretaries in the field of private and public administration is prevalent—yes, these social workers can tell how many people in your society wear this love-dress in the privacy of their homes and souls! I assure you that if you enter the minds, souls, and hearts of the majority of your respectable citizens, the only odor you will smell is the odor of selfishness, biological survival, envy, and violence. These are forces of hate and destruction. Moreover, if you examine the processes that microscopically and macroscopically constitute the structure of nature, you will discover that they are processes of change and that they will sooner or later cease to exist." Mowt stopped, took a deep breath, allowed a sarcastic smirk to hover at the corner of his mouth, and then continued, "I shall not bore you with examples, because you are a highly conversant scholar, but one more example should shed more light on my claim that the power of hate is greater than the power of love.

"Allow your imagination to leave the human world and stand on the peak of the highest mountain that overlooks the course of human civilization from its earliest stirrings to the present. Yes, stand on that peak and survey its course reflectively and critically, as you are wont to say—what does this course look like? You will agree with me that it looks like a series of rising and falling civilizations, empires, and cultures. Each one of them rises, reaches a peak of development or maturation, and then declines, sometimes fast and other times slowly. But they, and every newly emerging civilization, empire, and culture will eventually meet the same fate because this is the supreme law of the universe. Nothing endures, everything that comes into being will pass out of being! They rise by the power of love, that is, by the constructive power of human nature. But ask yourself, Dr. Athenaion, why is it that none of these civilizations, empires, and cultures continue to rise and continue to move to the highest point of perfection? This question may seem rhetorical. Nevertheless, I shall answer it for you. They do not endure, and they do not reach their point of perfection because, like a cancerous worm, the power of hate, of destruction, has been continually plotting and slowly undermining the accomplishments of the constructive power of love. Hate will never allow love to enjoy a moment of total victory. My uncle, the master of hate and destruction, was right when he said that nothing remains the same and that everything passes away except the ever-continuing process of change. But if nothing remains the same and everything is gradually moving into the abyss of nothing, then it should be easy to acknowledge that the power of hate and destruction is greater than the power of love and construction."

"On the contrary," Dr. Athenaion intervened, "this line of reasoning, as well as the examples you have provided, come from the mouth of a sophist. Your eyes can see the tree but not the forest. However, you cannot know or understand the tree if you do not know or understand the forest, and you cannot understand the forest as a whole unless you first understand who created it and why it was created. We understand an object only when we comprehend its cause or source. You seem to overlook a fundamental fact—"

"A fundamental fact?" Mowt interrupted, surprised.

"Yes, the fact that you, your uncle, and the universe are creatures—created beings! Love is the supreme creative power; *it is the ultimate power of creation and the source of everything that exists.* Any act of creation that aims at the good is an act of love, and the creation of the universe is the greatest act of love. Although the objects that make up the structure of the universe are continually changing, the universe endures. Its endurance reflects the triumph of love over hate, construction over destruction. Hate always lurks in the shadow of love, waiting to wreak havoc. Next, contrary to what you claim, although cultures, empires, and civilizations rise and fall, they do not only endure in the succeeding cultures, empires, and civilizations, they also inspire and, in fact, energize them to reach higher levels of perfection.

"A little while ago, you asked if I lifted my eyes toward The One. Now I ask, have *you* lifted your eyes toward The One? Again, have you asked yourself why you exist? But more importantly, have you noticed that you are a creature, which means that you are a created being, that you are an integral aspect of the universe, and that you exist as a part of the overall plan of the cosmic process? Although the objects comprising the fabric of the universe, be they atoms or mega galaxies, are continually changing, that is, continually coming into being and passing out of being, as I have just pointed out, the universe endures *because it is an emanation of The One* which you do not seem to comprehend. The One is the source of all being. It is an eternal and infinite source of being. It is the source of change as well as endurance. Have you asked yourself not only why The One created the universe, but why he created a universe that changes? Next, contrary to what you claim, although cultures, empires, and civilizations pass away, humanity in all its manifestations wings its way from the preceding cultures, empires, and civilizations like the fiery proverbial phoenix. I do not exaggerate when I say that the history of human civilization is a history of continual progress. Neither you nor anyone can deny this fact."

"Why do you and every object that exists pass away?"

"Because there is only one infinite, absolute being, The One. The universe and every object that emanates from it is finite. While the infinite is infinite in its creation and endures, the objects that emanate from it are necessarily temporal. Change is an essential aspect of finite beings. No one can change this aspect of their existence and destiny. You think and work on the assumption that passing out of existence, which your uncle calls perishing and which you call death, is evil, and you perpetrated this falsehood among people rather effectively. Have you perpetrated this falsehood as a means of manipulation, of inclining people to fear you and to obey you? As the creator of this amazing universe, The One is not only absolute in its creative power but also in its wisdom." Mowt was frowning, and his lips pursed when Dr. Athenaion made her last remarks.

"I understand your assertion that finite objects change, and that change is their essential aspect, but why do they change?" This question reached Dr. Athenaion as a challenge.

"You seem to ask the same question in different ways. The One ordained that change and perishing are the destiny of finite beings. It is obvious that you inflate the value of change and perishing unnecessarily. Does this reflect a selfish, and perhaps a narcissistic attitude? You remind me of the solipsist who is locked up in his minuscule self, sees the outside world with his minuscule eyes, and understands it with his minuscule mind. Unfortunately, your mind is not equipped with the power to get out of your minuscule self and experience and understand it from the standpoint of The One, from the standpoint of a human being who had a direct encounter with the Infinite One!"

"You give me the impression that you have spoken with him." The guest retorted sardonically.

"First, he is The Infinite. Therefore, he is not a kind of object. The category of 'object' does not apply to him. Accordingly, no one can speak with or about him. Second, although he is unspeakable, we can have an audience, and some would say an encounter with him. This kind of audience is possible in and through an experience of his emanation, which is the universe. I have a feeling that your logic is not as significant as you claim it to be."

"Arrogance is not one of your character traits, Dr. Athenaion!"

"Speaking the truth, so far as one comprehends it, is a radiant instance of modesty."

"I am beginning to change my opinion of you, Dr. Athenaion."

"Your opinion may be valuable to you, and you may esteem it highly, but am indifferent to it. I strongly feel that I have tolerated your intrusion, your impertinence, and your sophistry beyond the limits of courtesy. May I please ask you to—-"

"Not so fast, Dr. Athenaion! This is not our only visit."

"I am afraid it is."

"It cannot be! I am on a mission, and I intend to complete it."

"What is your mission?"

"To make sure that you abandon your work regarding the possibility of transforming contemporary society into a human community governed by technocrats. It is my plan to obstruct the development of this project. Any plan or project that fosters the progress of human ideals is a work of the God of Love. I loathe this god, and I loathe everything that comes from his heart and mind." Dr. Athenaion burst out laughing when she heard Mowt's intention.

"You are wasting my time. I advise you to see a psychiatrist as soon as possible."

"You must be mad!"

"What you say is ridiculous, to say the least," Dr. Athenaion said. And yet, an irresistible impulse inclined her to stare into his eyes. Her earlier question of who this creature is returned with compelling intensity. She felt a strong urge to know the identity of this unusual, inscrutable, yet seemingly real, human being. She could not suppress this impulse.

"Who are you?" she asked involuntarily.

"I am Mowt, the God of Death!" Dr. Athenaion pierced another sharp look into his eyes. He was real, and yet he was behaving as if he were a supernatural force. She was perplexed, not only because her curiosity intensified, not only because a streak of fear rocked the composure of her mind and heart, but especially because this extraordinary encounter was becoming a kind of nightmarish phenomenon. Without knowing how or why the idea that he was a supernatural force permeated her mind. This flicker of consciousness sent a shudder through every fiber of her being. "Oh, no, impossible!" she thought in the privacy of her mind. "We are in the twenty-first century, in the age of reason!"

"I shall not abandon my work on my project. Never! Neither you nor any other human being or power can deter me from working on it. May I please ask you to leave my apartment immediately!"

"I shall leave you immediately only because one of your students will be knocking at your door in a few minutes. In the meantime, I urge you to consider my request carefully, but more rationally than carefully. I shall pay you another visit as soon as I meet with some scholars in Germany. The Second World War has unfortunately transformed many of the philosophers in that country into a peace-loving community. That most destructive war, which I designed and engineered, produced undesirable side effects. I have to check these peace-loving tendencies!"

Dr. Athenaion did not know whether she was in the presence of a theater of the absurd performance or an actor in such a performance. But the guest, who noticed Dr. Athenaion's confusion and occasional absent-mindedness, for his eyes were able to see directly how she was feeling and what she was thinking, said, "I am the God of Death. If I were you, I would believe what I see, because as a god, I can assume the identity of any particular, or even general, human being. I can be visible and invisible, and I can behave like a god even when I appear in a human form. Sooner or later, you will be convinced that I am he, the God of Death."

"Sooner or later?" Dr. Athenaion blurted out as if she were trying to pull herself out of a thick, sticky puddle of mud.

"Yes, you should always remember that I am the nephew of the God of Hate and Destruction and that I am also the son of Abyss, the Infinite Void! Contrary to what you think, nothing escapes my attention in the realm of humanity. You should not decline my request because I usually achieve my purpose. I first employ the method of rational persuasion because human beings are dupes of reason, and philosophers are the greatest dupes on the face of the earth. They think that reason is God on earth—of course, only in their silly minds. For them, it is the source of truth and the basis of beauty, goodness, and wisdom. They are so arrogant, they are reluctant to recognize that, like all physical phenomena, what they call reason is an emergent, a product of the natural process and that it is such a product only because it is an effective means of survival. Yes, Dr. Athenaion, survival, human and natural, is the strongest motivator of everything human beings desire and hope for, and certainly not your mushy love or love of beauty, goodness, or truth. I have other methods of persuasion in store for realizing my purposes when or if the method of reason fails, as I hinted earlier."

"Other methods?" Dr. Athenaion asked rhetorically, surprise.

"Don't be surprised, and don't underestimate my powers. I am the most cunning and the most resourceful deity in my pantheon. I can make you and every other philosopher or artist comply with my request without much difficulty. Humanity is a race of weaklings!"

"What other methods?"

"Don't you think that a distinguished philosopher like you should know about the different methods of persuasion. I shall not directly answer your question, because doing so would be a grave insult to your intelligence."

"You do not insult me with your non-sensical conversation. You insult me with your very presence, with your intrusion into my privacy, with your insolence and your atrocious audacity."

"Yes, you are a truly accomplished human being and philosopher." The guest responded with the most resentful, most defiant, and most sardonic smile, and suddenly disappeared.

The guest's abrupt disappearance magnified Dr. Athenaion's confusion. Was he real? No. But he could not be unreal, she thought, because she was convinced without a shred of doubt that phantoms, gods, or any other type of supernatural beings did not exist. But then, how did he vanish from her presence without even saying goodbye, not to mention the supernatural behavior he exemplified when she agreed to welcome him as a guest a little while ago. She could not doubt her eyes, especially the fact that he was having a conversation with her! Regardless of his identity, why did he request that she abandon her work on the human community project? Is it possible for something to be and not to be at the same time and in the same place, to appear and disappear almost instantaneously? Was it possible for the most fundamental law of logic to tatter under his feet? "He must be real," she reasoned, "I remember every gesture, every movement, and every word he said. How did he vanish so suddenly? Is he a magician that was playing a trick on me? But even if he were one of those magicians we see on T.V. and some theaters, all the acts of sudden disappearance could be explained rationally, but this act was not in a theater or on T.V."

Two thick furrows formed on Dr. Athenaion's forehead. She found herself stuck between belief and disbelief. But, alas, how can one stand between these two antagonistic forces? Standing between them is like standing between being and non-being, between heaven and earth. This is tantamount to standing *nowhere*! Dr. Athenaion discovered existentially that one cannot think or act in that kind of place, which is no place! How can you speak with a person that exists and does not exist? How can you think even if you can speak to him? Dr. Athenaion was pulled out of this quandary by a knock at the door of her apartment. "Goodness! How did he know that someone would be knocking at the door?" She mumbled as she walked slowly to the door. Lo and behold, her most outstanding student in her Existentialism class greeted her with a polite, but cheerful, smile. She was pleased to see him and a few minutes later to discuss with him some of the central questions in Sartre's *Being and Nothing*.

But although she regained her sense of reality and treated her visit with her student as a celebration of *human existence*, Dr. Athenaion could not dismiss Mowt's reality, and unreality, from her mind. His threat that she abandon her work on the human community project surged into her consciousness when she placed her head on her pillow that night. She could not determine when she woke up the next morning, whether she did or did not sleep. It seemed to her that Mowt was becoming a permanent resident of her mind, not only during the day but also during the night.

CHAPTER TWO

A Look at The Athenaion Family

Dr. Athenaion was thirty-seven years old when Mowt intruded into her private life that morning. She was a highly esteemed professor at Union College and one of the academic luminaries in Jackson. She was loved by her students and respected by her colleagues. She was recognized for her logical and conceptual lucidity, depth of insight into the significant questions of philosophy, judicious comments in faculty meetings, and realistic understanding of the hardships and challenges faced by liberal education in a society that tends to value pleasure, success, security, money, and sex more than moral progress or a life of human growth and development. Moreover, Dr. Athenaion was acknowledged as a highly accomplished scholar in the realm of Metaphysics and Ethics. The University of Mississippi School of Medicine frequently invited her to deliver lectures on the nature of moral values and moral decision-making to the students, as well as to the faculty.

An accomplished teacher, scholar, faculty member, and human being is usually an object of jealousy and envy, but not Dr. Athenaion, for it was difficult, indeed impossible, to have or to display ill will toward such a person. How can you harm a person whose heart is a fountain of goodness? Would she return evil for evil? No. It would be appropriate to characterize such a person as a model of learning and human living and in what it means to be a human being. In fact, Dr. Athenaion was a model human being. She was described by her students and friends, privately and publicly, as "the best of the best"! In a conversation with the chair of the department of education, the dean of the college once remarked that we do not have, much less encounter, a professor like Dr. Athenaion in the various colleges and universities of the U.S. "It is difficult for me," he emphasized, "to decline any request or proposal she submits to me regardless of whether it relates to teaching, research, or the financial problems of the college. Students adore her! They rave about her. She is always rated higher than any member of the faculty. Union College is fortunate to have a professor like Dr. Anat Athenaion."

Also, Dr. Athenaion was a beautiful woman. She was elegant in the way she spoke, graceful in the way she walked, and seductive in the way she smiled. She did not use make-up. Neither her students nor her colleagues could resist the magnetic power of her character. Any aesthetically polished person could easily see that the charm of her beauty did not emanate merely from the harmony or comeliness her physique, although physically she was good-looking, but from something deeper, something that does not speak solely to the eyes and ears but to the soul, to the flame that sits at the base of our heart. There is a big difference between the beauty of the human body and the beauty of the person as a human being. Dr. Athenaion was a beautiful human being. Her beauty shone through her speech, the kind of ideas and values that infused the emotions she sought to express, and the way she behaved toward others. When she conversed with you, her body and speech became a living embodiment of the flame of life that glowed in her heart and mind.

I am not unaware of the made-up beauty that dominates the social marketplace. Such beauty is not genuine. It is a kind of mask people wear during their interaction with others in the different spheres of public life. It is generally weaved of sweet words, attractive clothes, facial paint, contrived styles of speaking, flattery, or the use of hundred-dollar words when they discuss a specific problem. Many people resort to made-up beauty mainly because it "sells." Notice how such people remove their beautiful masks the way they remove their coats when they go home after a visit, errand, or after a long day at the office. In contrast, genuine beauty flows from the moral heart spontaneously. I say "flows" because usually beautiful people are not aware of their beauty, and they do not try to be beautiful. They are beautiful, and they always seek to be their true selves! Does the beautiful fountain see that it is beautiful or that it is a fountain? Does the sun see its light? How can truly beautiful people stand before the mirror to see if they are beautiful? Who will they see there if they stand before that mirror? The fire of goodness and truth that flames in their hearts and minds? The beauty of the mind and the heart do not only add luster to the beauty of the body, but it also spiritualizes it and lifts it to a higher level of beauty!

Dr. Athenaion was the daughter of two high school teachers. Her father, Henry, taught history, and her mother, Dora, taught physics. They loved their daughter passionately, as they did every one of their four children. They exercised a profound influence on her social and academic growth. Once she remarked in my presence that her mother inspired her to inquire into the source and nature of the cosmic process, and her father inspired her to inquire into the basic structure of human nature and the nature of human growth and development. This twofold inspiration soon changed into an orientation, into a way of thinking, into a way of life. The main ideas she explored in her research and teaching revolved, directly and indirectly, around the nature of the world and human life: What is the source of this amazing spectacle of nature? What are the structure of human nature and the basis of the meaning of human life? She was convinced that an answer to the first question should shed ample light on how we should live.

The oldest of four children, Dr. Athenaion, had one sister, Felicity, and two brothers, Stanley and Kenny. Felicity was a practicing artist, and, like her parents, she was a teacher of art appreciation. Teaching was a means of living for her. But her deepest desire was to create artworks. She was especially interested in depicting the inner feelings, emotions, moods, and anxieties of people on canvas. She once mentioned that the spiritual world of people is the real world, not the outer world of social life, not the world of the madding crowd. This is where the real drama of human life unfolds. In a conversation with her mother one afternoon, she remarked that while her sister seeks to capture this drama through concepts, she seeks to achieve it through images.

Dr. Athenaion's older brother Stanley was an assistant professor of neurology at the University of Mississippi School of Medicine. He was intensely interested in artificial intelligence. His goal was to develop a model of artificial intelligence based on the essential structure of the human brain. The hypothesis he was trying to validate is that we should first identify the system of the various centers in the brain that perform the different human functions. Once we identify these centers and the dynamics that underlie their functioning, we should be able to devise artificial brains and techniques that expand our knowledge of the infinite possibilities of human knowledge and life. He frequently defended the feasibility and moral implication of his project with his older sister. One Sunday afternoon, after the family ate their dinner and gathered in the living room, as they always did, Dr. Athenaion asked her brother about his progress on the artificial intelligence project. He looked at her with reflective eyes and said, "The identification of the centers of the human functions in the brain, especially the dynamics of the interrelatedness and functions, is a challenge. But it is a sweet challenge. I tend to think that meeting this challenge, even if one fails, is a worthwhile endeavor."

"Both of you are dreamers," Kenny, who was listening to this exchange, intervened. "You cannot dream meaningfully if your feet are not tethered to the ground of reality. If you wish to expand your knowledge of human nature, the possibility of human growth and development, and especially what makes people tick in real life, you should enroll in a legal residency program for at least one year. Your laboratory should be offices of different types of legal practices, courtrooms, prisons, and the different legislative committees of the congress. No one can theorize adequately about human nature unless they first explore in some detail this domain of human experience."

"Has it occurred to you, Kenny," Dr. Athenaion responded, "that, contrary to what you and many thinkers seem to assume, neither the philosopher nor the scientist is a dreamer or permanent residents of an ivory tower. They go to those towers only after they have *immersed* their minds, hearts, and souls in the stream of practical life, that is, in the different dimensions of human experience. This immersion is the basis of their theorizing in those towers. They reflect on the mystery of nature, the source of humanity, and the dynamics of the different types of human desires, capacities, and aspirations. They reflect on the dynamics of the struggle of people in their effort to meet their needs and be happy with the pain, frustration, triumphs, and failures they face in this struggle. They reflect on the conditions under which human beings can create a better world. How can they pursue these purposes, and much more, if they have not first seen, felt, and understood the reality of human existence as it unfolds throughout history? I fully agree with you they should do legal residencies and other types of internships to reach a realistic understanding of the actuality of human life before they withdraw for a while to their ivory towers."

"We should make a distinction between real philosophers, those who philosophize, and who are few, and philosophy teachers and technicians, that is, those who communicate, interpret, and comment on the ideas of real philosophers. The real philosopher is one who seeks to intuit *the meaning of nature and human nature and articulate it into a conceptual framework the way Michelangelo intuited David in a slab of marble and articulated his essence in a beautiful image."*

"You are a most lovable sister," Kenny cried when he heard this clarification of the task of the philosopher, which applies to the scientist, as Stanley confessed, "but the point I wish to underscore is that we cannot identify the various centers of the human functions in the brain if we do not proceed in our inquiry from a clear conception of the different dimensions of human nature. How can we look for something if we do not know what we are looking for?"

"I agree with you," Dr. Athenaion retorted, "that an adequate conception of human nature cannot be based *solely* on the findings of neuroscience, the social sciences, the theologian, or the physicist but the knowledge provided by all the thinkers from different realms of human experience. The investigative eye of the inquirer should observe how people think, feel, desire, hope, value, enjoy beauty, love, hate, and how they pursue happiness. In short, the process of inquiry, and consequently of theorizing, should begin from the bottom up, not from the top down. You need a god's mind that can comprehend all these types of knowledge into a coherent whole. Moreover, we should treat this type of knowledge as complementary, not as exclusive of each other."

"You seem to assume that human nature is kind of a given, definable essence or reality and that we can place it under the microscope of one or a group of thinkers. If you do, your view will simultaneously be a one-sided and short-sighted assumption—yes, assumption, no more. But as you know, all assumptions and or claims require verification. However, before you proceed to this verification, ask yourself: Is it an essence? What kind of reality is it? We cannot close the domain of inquiry before be we begin our inquiry."

"Yes, we should recognize any type of thinker who sees and understands human nature from a certain perspective."

"And the historian?" Henry asked in an attempt to expand the field of inquiry. "I emphasize the field of history because history is a kind of mirror that reflects the essential fabric of human nature. We can say that the history of civilization is *Human Nature-Writ-Large*. Don't we see every type of human experience, feeling, emotion, capacity, desire, aspiration, belief, and ideal, in short, everything that pertains to our humanity represented in this extraordinary narrative? Let me rush to add that by human civilization,

I do not merely mean the narration of the events that make up the plot of history—oh, no! I mean the living reality of history in the mind of the inquirer into the basic structure of human nature, I mean comprehension of its achievements in the different areas of human life. How can you understand the history of a past society if you do not comprehend its religion, science, philosophy, art, culture, political system, and its worldview? That is, if you do not enter its mind, heart, and soul, if you do not comprehend how it lived according to its understanding of itself and the world?"

"Thank you for this important contribution to our conversation, Father!" Dr. Athenaion said. "We may view history as a kind of framework, or a comprehensive field, of inquiry in which we can explore and identify the various dimensions of human experience. Accordingly, no inquirer into the basis and structure of human nature can neglect a type of human experience represented in this field—would you agree?" Dr. Athenaion asked, looking at her brother and the rest of the family expectantly.

"No one can afford to disagree with your father, my dear," her mother said with a smile frolicking on her lips.

"If we agree with our father," Stanley interjected, "then we can assert that every type of human experience reflects a certain type of human function. For example, we can speak of religious, aesthetic, intellectual, and social functions, each of which is performed by a brain center. The task of the neuroscientist is to explore the nature of each one of these and other centers."

"But," Stanley continued, "if we can locate the human functions in brain centers, then we have *ipso facto* discovered the ontic basis of human nature because an understanding of these centers, that is, their capacities, possibilities, and dynamics would be tantamount to an adequate conception of human nature. It seems to me that such a conception would be an effective principle of explanation—of what it means to be a human being."

"You imply that such a conception will explain all the features, capacities, and dynamics of human nature, for example, creativity in science, philosophy, practical life, and technology; the urge to ask questions concerning the reason for being of natural and human existence in general, and human existence in particular; confronting the mystery that permeates human life; the desire to seek the ultimate; the emotions of love, hate, hope, and loneliness; the need for art and aesthetic appreciation; the capacity to wonder about the baffling mystery of self-consciousness; the desire for happiness; and other features we usually attribute to human nature," Dr. Athenaion reasoned.

"Yes, I imply all this. It seems to me, sister, that the scientific method is the royal road to an adequate knowledge of nature and humanity. It may not now have answers to all the questions you mentioned and to several other mysteries. But I think it will slowly but surely unlock the secrets of all the enigmas, puzzles, and recalcitrant questions that challenged the human mind over the past centuries."

"I admire your optimism, Stanley," Kenny said, "but let us focus our attention on the phenomenon of human nature for a moment. You argued, Anat, that the different dimensions of human experience are functions and capacities inherent in human nature, and Stanley argued that these capacities are inherent in centers in the brain. Therefore, if we arrive at adequate knowledge of these centers, we shall have solved the problem of the basis of human nature. But the central question of this conversation is, 'What is human nature?' When we say that the different types of human experience are capacities inherent in human nature or that, they are functions of specific brain centers, we imply that a certain reality, of which these types of experience are functions, exists. Something must be inherent in these centers or capacities: What is this something?"

"As a scientist, I can explore the existence of different centers in the brain responsible for the different types of human experience, but I cannot envision a center that is called or can be the source of something we may call 'human nature.' All I can say is that when we speak of human nature, we refer to these centers and functions and nothing else."

"Do you mean that the possibility of discovering *a network of centers* founded in a reality called 'human nature' is not a viable hypothesis?"

"It will be a serious hypothesis, but a farfetched one."

"Why?"

"Because it will throw us in the snare of Cartesianism, which is tantamount to replacing the category of 'spirit,' or soul, by the category of matter. However, this kind of approach is simplistic."

"But is its logic weak or simplistic?"

"What do you mean?"

"I mean that if we posit a diversity of brain centers that are responsible for the different types of human functions, then we can ask, 'What makes them human?' Or, under what conditions, if such conditions can be articulated or identified, can we say a particular function is human? It seems to me that an answer to this question is urgently needed. Otherwise, any reference to these centers would be arbitrary. But characterizing them, or any of them arbitrarily would be a mistake, if not misleading."

"Why?" Stanley intervened.

"Because a reasonable conception of humanity is not only needed but is also logically implied in any significant pursuit we undertake in our theoretical lives. Indeed, any such pursuit is justified on the ground that it is human. What is the aim of the artist in creating an artwork, the scientist in hypothesizing on a specific aspect of the world, the legislator in repealing or enacting a new law, or the social reformer in advocating for a certain social agenda *but* the promotion of the human growth and development of our humanity? What justifies our attempt to define good and evil, right and wrong, and beauty and ugliness but the promotion of human wellbeing? *But can we promote human wellbeing if we do not know what makes us human*?"

"Don't you think, sister," Stanley interjected, "that if we understand the basics and dynamics of the centers in the brain that perform the human functions, we can use this understanding as a platform for designing the future activities in our personal and public lives?"

"Yes, but how can we arrive at a comprehensive and adequate understanding of these functions if we do not proceed in this task from a reasonably articulated conception of humanity? I am afraid, Stanley, that the articulation of such a conception cannot be undertaken by the empirical scientist primarily because the scientific method is designed to explore only the directly given facts, or those that are necessarily implied by them, nor all the facts of human life. It is not designed to explore why they exist or the basis of their existence, nor can it explain the basis of human values. Even if everything, including human beings, in this universe, forms an integral part of nature, and this is an agreeable hypothesis, it does not necessarily follow that everything that exists is reducible to directly given objects. Let me introduce the concept of creativity to the realm of our conversation—" Unaware of what was happening around her, Dr. Athenaion was interrupted by the voice of her father saying, "We need a short break. Your mother is brewing a pot of coffee. We cannot deprive her of this part of our conversation, especially your forthcoming remarks on creativity. We should be ready for a sip of coffee, anyway."

What Henry said was followed by heaving chests. Apparently, the family was deeply engrossed in the interchange between Stanley and his sister. "You are right, Father," Kenny remarked, "the subject of this conversation is, as my sister emphasized, essentially pertinent to what we all do. Our lives and the lives of all human beings will, I think, be more satisfying if we recognize that our work is substantially significant."

"Yes," Felicity seconded her brother, "particularly artists! I emphasize this point only because our society tends to marginalize art as if this type of activity is indispensable to human happiness or progress."

"Yes, my dear," her mother, who was standing behind her, said in support of her daughter. She was carrying a tray of demitasse cups of coffee. She distributed the cups and sat next to her husband.

"Creativity?" Stanley asked after his mother was seated next to Henry.

"Yes, nature is not a scheme of given, or ready-made objects, but is instead a process. Everything that exists is continually changing, regardless of whether it is a grain of sand, and electron, a mountain, or a galaxy. No matter its kind, nothing lingers. This is a generally recognized fact by philosophers, scientists, and artists, even by ordinary people. But what is not recognized by people, in general, is that as a process of change, nature is a *creative process*, a continual advance into higher levels of being. This phenomenon is not restricted to the cosmic levels of being but noticeably includes all the levels of being, especially in the domain of the human race. The conditions of survival, or existence, are constantly changing. Accordingly, a creative response to this change is a necessary condition for survival. The organism must adapt to the new conditions of survival and transform it into a livable environment. A plant that cannot adjust to the unique elements of its environment, for example, drought, heat, wind, or floods, will necessarily perish, as will the animal in the wild, as well as human beings when they are assaulted by a deadly virus. But the demand for a higher and more refined measure of creativity in the human species is higher primarily because, although they are animals, they have advanced into a higher level of being—humanity. This type of being is unique and cannot be reduced to natural terms.

"Humanity is not, as I shall explain presently, given as a natural object the way trees or rocks are given, that is, it is not presented as a ready-made reality. It comes into being in a creative response to a demand inherent in human nature. During this activity, the various dimensions of humanity—thinking, feeling, self-consciousness, and willing—come into being. Not one of these dimensions is given to us as ready-made at birth. What is given is the potentiality to think, to feel, to be self-conscious, and to make decisions. The realization of these potentialities is a continuous process of creation. We learn how to be creative, therefore, how to grow as human beings in different educational, religious, social, cultural, and political institutions. For example, we realize the capacity to think and create new ideas, to appreciate art and create artworks, or to love and be loved as we grow up. The extent to which we can become creative in realizing the human potential varies from one individual to another and from one cultural environment to another.

"But humanity cannot exist divorced from nature, that is, the body, nor can it be understood separate from it. I would not be amiss if I characterize nature as its home," Stanley pointed out.

"Certainly. But from the fact that humanity, as such, is emergent from nature or that it is anchored in it, it does not necessarily follow that it can be understood by the categories of the established scientific methods. I am convinced that not one of the empirical sciences has attempted to reform or reconstruct their methods in a way that accommodates an adequate explanation of the activities of this emergent. The sciences concern themselves with the given realm of reality—the realm of sensual facts. But the realm of humanity is not given directly as a realm of facts. It is the realm of *human values, of human meaning.* Meaning is not a public fact; it is a subjective datum of experience. But although it is subjective, and so exists in the experience of the individual, it can nevertheless be an intersubjective datum in intersubjective experience. Otherwise, neither this conversation nor any type of communication in science, art, social life, religion, would be possible at all. During the past several centuries, the different thinkers in the different areas of the humanities have been perfecting the conditions under which intersubjectivity in the different areas of knowledge is possible."

"The point meriting particular emphasis now is that the realm of meaning is the realm of values— religious, intellectual, aesthetic, social, political, moral, and personal values. As you know, values are general concepts; we sometimes refer to them as ideals. A value realized in experience is a value transformed into an experience of meaning. The medium in which it is realized is feeling—the feeling of the individual who realizes it.

"People belong to two worlds, the world of nature and the world of humanity. Like plants and animals, human beings seek to survive at the level of the body. This type of survival is a fundamental urge in nature and human nature since humanity is emergent from nature. But the survival of the human being as a human reality is also a basic urge in human nature. This *urge manifests itself as basic needs*. For example, this includes the need to love and be loved, to enjoy beautiful things, to seek the company of other human beings, to respond to the mystery of nature, or to be happy. Each one of these needs points to or is associated with a value. This is the main reason why I said that the realm of meaning is the realm of values, and this is why I can now say that, at the practical level, human beings live in the realm of values, even when they endeavor to meet their biological needs, because in whatever they do they action based on some value, that is, based on a religious, aesthetic, intellectual, or social value. Don't we endeavor to beautify our homes (shelter)? Don't we try to make our food tasty? Don't we try to wear beautiful clothes? In short, don't we try to transform the natural environment into a system of artifacts? The human eyes do not merely see the mountain or the river, or the sunset, they also see them as beautiful or good, or as a manifestation of the Creator of the Universe. Doesn't the musician hear the wind, the running water, the howling of the animals or the silence of the night and express their essence in artistic form? Although human beings form part of nature, live in it, and view it as their home, it is a *built environment, and it is built in their image*!

"Many people view philosophers and scientists as intellectual adversaries, but, my dear sister, I do not view you as my adversary. On the contrary, I see you as my collaborator in a quest of the ontic basis of human nature. You must be an evolutionary philosopher. This discovery pleases my scientific heart immensely—"

"You can also characterize me as a process philosopher because, in its attempt to explain the various phenomena of the universe, this kind of philosophy begins where the empirical scientist stops. The process philosopher does not merely assume but also incorporate 'emergence' as an underlying assumption in their analysis of the meaning of the world and human life."

"Great! Let me then ask, '*What type of reality steps into the actual world when human nature emerges from the womb of nature*?' You are right. As a scientist, I investigate observable phenomena, and as a neuroscientist, I investigate the human brain as a phenomenon in so far as it is perceptible by the scientific method of thinking and investigation. But, as you have just explained to us, albeit briefly, human nature is not a directly observable phenomenon, and yet, we know it as a kind of reality because, as you have discussed, we experience and live what *it does and creates*."

"If human nature is not a physical reality, and yet emerges from the womb of nature," Kenny interjected, "under what condition does it emerge?"

"I shall try to answer this question on two conditions."

"What are your conditions?"

"First, I shall be brief only because this is a huge and controversial subject, and, second, I shall assume the most recent findings in the biological sciences and the humanities." Kenny, his sister, Felicity, and his parents nodded.

"We accept your conditions. Frankly, we are interested primarily in the fundamental elements of your thesis. We can discuss the details later if we have to."

"Fine! Let me first submit that the kind of reality we call 'human nature' is essentially a power, *dynamis*. But it is different from the types of power we encounter in nature primarily because it is an *originative source*, a root. It inheres in the brain as a potentiality and comes into being, into life, when a person becomes self-conscious or when they wake up from sleep. Humanity emerges as a function of self-consciousness. We exist as human beings in so far as we are conscious of ourselves and the world around us or when we feel responsible for what we do or when we are in charge of the actions we perform. When we sleep, or when we lose our minds, we cease to be real human beings. We exist and function as humans when we are responsive to our needs. In a state of sleep, we are potential human beings. We cannot think, feel, or act at the human level. How can we perform our human function in this state? How can we be treated as human beings if we do not act like human beings? Is this why we cannot interact with the lower animals? Is this why nurses, doctors, even family members do not interact existentially or seriously with comatose people, although they show signs of respect and sometimes love for them? Don't we celebrate with smiles and cheers when a comatose person regains their consciousness after a long coma? Emergence from a coma signifies the emergence of consciousness. It also signifies the emergence of the humanity of the comatose person. Here, I assume that the impetus of this emergence is a primary locus, or a point of origin, or a source, which inheres in the brain as a potentiality. Its rise activates the other human centers. They become active only because they exist as a network, for one cannot function without the proper functioning of the others. For example, the act of knowledge involves the ability to perceive, relate, remember, conceive, judge, generalize, imagine, and comprehend. Again, the function of hate, or hating, involves the capacity to remember, feel, know, emote, desire, and recognize. In themselves, the activities of the different human functions in the brain, singly or cooperatively, are passive. They are administered by a 'subject' that designs and steers them according to a purpose, for example, knowledge, love, or hate. This subject, which has so far eluded the scientific method, but not necessarily the scientist as a thinker, is the *seat of self-consciousness* without which neither personal identity nor acts of knowledge or any intellectual or spiritual activity, is possible at all."

"This subject exists in the brain as a unique potentiality. The distinguishing aspect of this uniqueness is the capacity of self-consciousness. I should underline this point because human beings act as a subject by virtue of this capacity. If you deprive people of self-consciousness, you deprive them of their humanity. It is an indispensable condition for the activities of thinking, feeling, and willing. Can we perform any of these activities if we are not conscious of what we are doing? Again, can we recognize what we are doing if we do not know that we are the authors of what we are doing? But what makes this capacity especially significant is that it is the source of all the spiritual activity, and consequently of the beliefs and values that underlie everything we desire or pursue throughout our daily lives. We do not only see the sunset and know that it is a sunset, but we also see it as beautiful. We do not only experience nature as infinite, mysterious, and an extension of our being, we also question why it exists. We witness a person suffering from devastating disease and know what it means to suffer, we also sympathize with them and condemn this suffering as evil. We see a person taking the handbag of an old woman by force, but we also say that this person stole the handbag. We may view these beliefs and values as the building blocks of the human dimension of our being, primarily because they are the instruments by which we grow in our humanity. The more they are refined conceptually and logically, and the more they are realized in our lives, the more we grow in our humanity."

"I do not exaggerate when I say that these beliefs and values humanize not only our bodies, not only our environment but also our very selves because they help us to transform the means of living, as well as our environment, into our human image. The houses we live in are not merely shelters; they are also beautiful objects and conducive to human growth and development. The food we eat is not merely a means of survival, it is also tasty and conducive to longevity. The clothes we wear are not merely a means of protecting our bodies from hot and cold weather or to secure modesty, they are also aesthetically pleasing objects. Moreover, when I stand before a family member, a friend, or a neighbor, even a stranger, I do not stand before a lump of flesh, I stand before a human reality because this so-called lump of flesh is a humanized being. It radiates its humanity in the way it walks, speaks, responds to me when I speak, and the way it conducts its life. In short, the natural environment, in which we are anchored by means of our bodies, is not raw nature but a built environment, even when it extends before our vision as an infinite sea, deep valley, high mountain, or dense forest. Don't we see them in terms of the way we know and value them? What are the instruments by which we humanize our lives and environment, *but* the beliefs and values that make up the structure of our humanity?" More than once, Kenny tried to intervene by raising his hand, but his sister interrupted his interventions with 'One moment, brother, please! "

"The dwelling within which our humanity grows is self-consciousness. The first flicker of this activity is 'consciousness' of something. Although this something is a particular type of object, a tree, a cat, an idea, or my hand, it is at once an implied act of self-consciousness: consciousness of X. Knowing that one is conscious of X, implies self-consciousness. I cannot be conscious of the tree as an object out there if I am not simultaneously conscious of myself as perceiving this very tree. The human self steps into the realm of reality by means of this activity. Self-consciousness is assumed in every act of knowledge. It entitles us to claim authorship of what we know and do. Isn't the 'I' implied in every cognitive expression we make? How can I, for example, say that this paper is white or that the world is infinite or finite if I do not know, or at least imply, that I am the author of my statement?"

"It is essential to point out that the concept of self-consciousness is *paradoxical* because it implies that the subject, which perceives or knows the object as an 'other,' becomes an *object to itself* yet remains the subject of its experience. How can a subject be its object at the same time and in the same event, that is, how can it be subject and object simultaneously? We may or may not be able to answer this question, but what matters, from a phenomenological point of view, is that we cannot be the subject and object of our own experiences. We can only imply, and the implication is logical, that we can be the subject and object at the same time because it is a fact that we know we are the author of specific experience and that we are aware of this cognitive act. "

"You have argued that human nature exists as a potentiality in the individual brain," Kenny was finally able to intervene," that it emerges as a subject when the human organism becomes conscious of itself, and that the humanizing forces of the subject are beliefs and values, and that these beliefs and values are the building blocks of the human dimension of the human individual. What is the ontological status of the subject or the human dimension? What is its stuff? Is it physical in character? If it is not, how is it related to the body? How do you avoid the dualism that had plagued the multitude of views on human nature since the days of Plato?"

"Let me say, considering what I have just said, that the human being is the concrete physical person I encounter in the real world—you, my sister, my parents, and my brother, as well as the people I meet in the marketplace. This very person, and nothing else, is what I mean by 'human being.' It is an embodiment of humanity. It is a multidimensional reality. The man with whom I am now speaking behaves as a thinker, a few moments later, he will behave as my brother, tomorrow morning when he goes to his office he will behave as a lawyer, and when he walks in the streets of Jackson, he will behave as a citizen. He is all these *personae* because each is an instantiation of the human dimension, one made up of individual beliefs and values and founded in the brain as a potentiality."

"Although this human being is a lump of flesh, it is a *human* lump of flesh, and it is human by virtue of possessing particular centers in the brain. The unity of these centers represents the ontic basis of the structure of humanity. Every organism, regardless of its shape or size, that possesses these centers is entitled to membership to the human race. They fundamentally underscore communication and association as friends, families, communities, and societies."

"When we speak of emergence," Kenny pressed on, "we mean the coming into being of some kind of reality. But as a capacity, human nature is different from any other capacity in the brain because the powers and functions of humanity transcend the brain in which it is embedded. For example, the capacity for breathing air or digesting food is restricted to the dimension of the body, but not the capacity for thinking, feeling, and willing. You speak of the subject as if it is autonomous as if the body is under its dominance."

"Yes, it is autonomous so far as its nature allows. It cannot violate the laws of nature, the same laws that govern the functions of the animal organism. For example, it cannot fly or carry a mountain on its back, nor can it violate the laws of its own nature. For example, we cannot accept any proposition as valid if it is contradictory, and we cannot accept anything as ugly if it is aesthetically beautiful, we cannot accept any act as good if it is harmful or if it impedes human satisfaction or progress.

"The emergence of the human being as a subject, when it opens its eyes to its environment, that is when that flicker of self-consciousness introduces the individual to the world, is the emergence of a *humanized body*, a body that exists in a human world and whose life happens to unfold in it. The human capacity for thinking, feeling, and willing *qua* subject performs the activity of living the way the *capacity* for breathing, for example, performs the *function* of breathing."

"Do you imply that the human function is a natural function? Is it a brain function that is reducible to physico-chemical processes?"

"It is natural in so far as it is embedded in the brain, but its activity is not reducible to physico-chemical processes—"

"Why?"

"Because what emerges in a state of consciousness is not matter nor a direct extension of the brain the way the messages that are sent to a certain organ from a brain center through the nervous system are extensions of the brain. What emerges is a unique reality. Although this reality remains a part of the brain and remains an emanation from it, it is different from the material structure from which it emerges. Don't we feel the sadness of the face in the sad face yet the sadness is not a part of the physical structure of the face, and in general, don't we feel the humanity of the stranger that sits next to us in the bus in the body next to which we sit? When I embrace my beloved with my arms and hold her to my bosom warmly, do I embrace a lump of flesh or a lump of flesh that radiates humanity? Similarly, don't we feel the depth of the human enigma in DaVinci's *Mona Lisa,* yet the enigma is not a part of the canvas? When I say that the subject humanizes the human body, I mean that the subject that resides in the brain is, to speak metaphorically, like a flame, a spirit, a light that permeates the whole body primarily because it energizes it according to its mind and will! Moreover, this unique reality, which I have so far called the subject, is the source of the capacity of transcendence, that is, of transcending the body and, indeed, steering it, of course, according to the laws of nature. It is also the source of self-consciousness. It enables the human organism to will modes of action that are not direct functions of the brain, primarily because its basis is not the physical activity of the brain but the beliefs and values it has acquired throughout its life-experience. Human beings can create ideas and values and act according to them. These beliefs and values are not chemical processes. Their experience cannot be understood via the categories of physics or chemistry. They are peculiarly human in character.

Let me, at this point, hasten to add that the domain of beliefs and values is infinite because the human potential is an inexhaustible wealth of creation, and so of realization."

"It should follow from the preceding line of reasoning that although the human dimension does not exist separate from the brain, it cannot exist apart from it—correct?"

"Yes! Now, allow me to remark that the dynamics that underlie the emergence of the human dimension from the activity of the brain are one of the most amazing, most mysterious, and indeed most miraculous aspects of the cosmic process. It is only a clear indication of the secret of its creativity. Scientists, like my brother Stanley, may one day focus their investigative effort on how that which is material can give rise to something that transcends the bounds of matter!"

"It should also follow that when the brain cannot perform its human function, it ceases to be a human brain—correct?"

"Yes!"

"Is it time for questions?" Felicity asked.

"Yes!" Dr. Athenaion said with a smile on her lips. "It is always open to questions!"

"Your hypothesis on the ontic status of human nature is, to my mind, provocative. I am sure that Stanley and our parents are anxious to ask you questions, but I shall raise one before I yield the floor. It has been on my mind for some time."

"I hope it is not my question!" Kenny intervened, teasingly.

"If it is, so much, the better! Does your view undermine religion? Can one be religious without believing in some kind of soul entity?"

"It undermines belief in such a soul entity, but it does not undermine genuine religion or being religious. Religion essentially denotes a relationship between the individual and God. Accordingly, one can commune with God without necessarily believing in a soul. Moreover, being religious is independent of belief in heaven, hell, or a type of supra-natural domain."

"One more question, if no one objects?"

"No one objects," Henry said, coming to the rescue of his daughter.

"Some people think that human beings are bad by nature. But this belief seems to be implied by the way people are brought up, the way they interact with each other, and the extent to which their lives happen to be happy or miserable. For example, those who lie, cheat, act selfishly, and hypocritically seem to be more, much more, than those who act compassionately, generously, justly, trustworthily, and courageously. 'Be careful!' is always on the lips of our parents, husbands, wives, friends, and teachers. Why is this advice an integral part of practical thinking and behaving? Why is true friendship rare? Why do we need jails and police protecting the streets of our cities? Why do we need law courts? Why do we lock our doors when we are away from our homes and when we go to sleep? I can cite many more examples, but is human nature bad? If it is, how can we qualify it with the quality of badness?"

"Yes, sister, you have stolen my question," Kenny said with a flare of gladness in his eyes. "An answer to this question should not only enlighten us but also show whether Anat's hypothesis is defensible."

"Let me first say this," Dr. Athenaion began, "in itself, human nature is neither good nor bad. People possess the tendency to act good or bad, and this tendency exists as a potentiality in their individual nature. Acting as good depends on the extent to which they are educated or the extent to which they have matured intellectually, emotionally, and practically, while acting badly depends on the extent to which they are deprived of the opportunity to grow emotionally, intellectually, and practically. If we grant, as we should, that certain beliefs and values are the building blocks of human nature and that they form the basis of its realization in the life of the individual, if these beliefs and values are the basis for action, then the goodness or badness of an action will depend on the extent to which it is performed according to valid, true, or genuine beliefs and values. Here, I assume that an action performed according to genuine and true beliefs or values would be good, while one performed according to false or spurious beliefs and values would be bad. The goodness or badness of an action is determined by the kind of beliefs and values we act on and the extent to which we act on them wisely. Was it an accident that the master of Western philosophy said that ignorance is the source of evil?

"But if beliefs and values form the basis for action, if they originate from a will that aims at the good and avoids the bad, then it should follow that the practical key to an adequate understanding of goodness and badness in human life is *education*. The ingredients of this type of education are sound judgment and a firm moral sense. The medium of this education should not be restricted to academic or school education but should include the family and the major institutions within which people grow and undertake the business of human living. The aims of education are the cultivation of *human character* and *preparing the young for practical life*. I emphasize the first aim only because I firmly believe that it should be a necessary condition for the second: a good human being will be a good professional. A person armed with enlightened, rational faculties and a living moral sense will most likely act responsibly in all the spheres of their lives.

"Moreover, it is critically important to emphasize that the question of good and evil is not merely a question of inquiring into the concept of moral goodness, regardless of whether the inquirer is a philosopher or a theologian, but also *of being good* or the conditions under which a person can be good. The second question presupposes the first. One may possess extensive knowledge of good and bad without necessarily being good or bad. But the point meriting our express attention is the conditions under which one can be good or can grow in goodness. Good people *act morally* because *they are good*. Their actions flow from a moral, or good, heart, and their moral hearts shine in their good actions. Some people act *as if* they are good without necessarily being good. For example, a person may donate some money to a charity, not from a generous heart, but because the donation fosters his social image or business. But the point is *to be good, to live from a good heart*."

"Then, can we say that goodness is an achievement?"

"Yes."

"If, as you say, education is the most effective means of cultivating human character, how should we view the many people who are, for some reason, deprived of the right kind of education?" Felicity asked.

"Let me, first, say that the institution of the right system of education has always been a challenge and a struggle, as you and our parents know better than any of us. Second, we should treat those who are deprived of the education they deserve as human beings with respect, tolerance, support, and generosity of spirit. We commit a grave mistake if we disenfranchise them politically, economically, socially, or in any other way. This statement assumes that the human spark, the spark that defines our humanity and which is common to all of us, *is sacred*. We are equal in our humanity, even though we are not equal in our social, intellectual, cultural, or economic endowments or achievements—"

"How about self-creation? What if a person loses a spouse after many years of good, or even bad, marriage because of death, divorce, or some calamity—can such a human being re-create themself?"

"Certainly! As I emphasized earlier, human nature, in its intellectual, moral, social, aesthetic, and cultural dimensions, is an inexhaustible wealth of potentialities, of resources. Self-creation, or re-creation, is not easy, for many psychological, social, and material reasons. Still, it is in principle quite possible, and I daresay that most people are skillful in the art of self-creation. Don't we constantly, in realizing the kind of projects we pursue, create ourselves? Isn't it our obligation to create and continue to re-create ourselves primarily because we are born in order to live? But how can we live if we do not create and constantly re-create ourselves? Self-creation is the essence of human life! Again, if human life is a thrust into the future, if the future does not yet exist, then it should follow that our life is a goal, a goal to be realized. What is this realization but an activity of creation? We can be efficient or inefficient in achieving this goal, and we can be brilliant or mediocre. But regardless of how we achieve it, it always involves a measure of creation, even when we do it routinely."

"Do you think," Felicity pressed on, tongue in cheek, "that the value of goodness will, at some point in the future, prevail over badness?"

"Yes."

"What is the source of your optimism?"

"Based on my metaphysical meditations, I can say that the cosmic process is constructive in nature. The emergence of the values of goodness, truth, and beauty is a strong indication that the world is gradually moving toward a higher state of being. Otherwise, how can we explain the gradual evolution of human culture into this stunning spectacle of science, philosophy, politics, art, and economics that does not seem to slow down but, on the contrary, to grow in vitality and creativity?"

Henry intervened at this juncture of the conversation. "We have burdened Anat beyond the limit of courtesy," he said, "we can discuss this question next Sunday. Actually, Anat provoked many questions in my mind about education, the relation between science and the humanities, and especially the ontic status of human nature. I would very much appreciate the discussion of these and related questions! In the meantime, how about a glass of sherry?"

"I second that suggestion, Father," Felicity said. "Anat deserves two glasses of sherry."

"Yes, she does!" Dora said.

CHAPTER THREE

Henry Athenaion's Last Testimony

"Your sister called a few minutes ago. She needs to see you now," Julie, Dr. Athenaion's assistant, said the moment Dr. Athenaion walked into her office. Surprised, because her sister rarely called her during the day, she impulsively asked:

"My sister?" She asked, still standing next to her desk.

"Yes, your sister, Felicity." The surprise which shone from Dr. Athenaion's eyes a few moments ago froze on her face and slowly crept into her heart. "She seemed agitated," Julie added.

"Agitated?" Dr. Athenaion returned, wide-eyed.

"Yes, she was adamant that you call her immediately—-"

"Immediately?" Dr. Athenaion interrupted Julie again, hastily.

"As soon as possible. These are her words."

Mystified, Dr. Athenaion threw a thoughtful look at her assistant and then walked silently to her chair. Julie, who realized that she had delivered a disturbing message to her favorite professor and always protected her privacy, returned to her desk, which was located near the door, and said, "I shall be back shortly, Dr. Athenaion."

"Thank you, Julie!" Dr. Athenaion said distractedly as Julie left the office with a file in her hand.

But Dr. Athenaion did not call her sister, not because she was selfish, apathetic, or busy, nor because she did not take the message Julie conveyed to her seriously, but because she was seized by an overwhelming feeling of apprehension. This feeling was accompanied, perhaps caused by a swarm of questions. "Why? "she asked. "What might be the cause of her agitation?

She cannot be sick because she just called from her office. Is she having a problem with Norman, her boyfriend? Is there some kind of conflict between her and the Principal or a colleague?" These and a host of other questions coursed frantically through her mind, and they seemed to provoke more questions than she could answer or consider. Although she tried to ignore them, she could not because new questions continued to rush in.

We usually feel apprehensive when we discover that the people we love profoundly are in serious trouble. We also feel that we cannot remain idle. On the contrary, we try to do everything we can to help them. This seems to be a natural reaction, and in fact, this was how Dr. Athenaion felt when Julie told her that her sister was agitated and that she needed to speak with her immediately. But, for some mysterious reason, no-one could understand, she was in the grip of those questions against her will. She had always been able to control the flow of ideas and feelings entering and exiting her mind, but not that afternoon. More than once, she tried to call her sister, but she could not even extend her arm to pick up the telephone. She felt powerless. She tried to extricate herself from this state of sudden impotence but to no avail. She felt that a mysterious force was steering the passage, even grip, of the questions that were swarming her mind. She also felt that this same force was seizing her will in a stubborn grasp as if to suffocate it. What baffled her most was her inability to free herself from that grip. Have you ever been in a physical and psychological straight-jacket, dear reader? In such a jacket, you do not only lose control of your body, because you cannot move, but you also lose control of your mind, because you lose command of your ideas and decision-making capacity. When you know you are in this kind of jacket, and you cannot do anything about it, you feel incensed, and if you cannot be stoic about it, you feel debilitated.

Fortunately, Dr. Athenaion was stoic about it and did not remain in that straight-jacket for long because the telephone rang. An inner power, one rooted in the vital impetus of human nature, splintered that jacket into nothing. She picked up the phone impulsively without having either the interest or the time to reflect on the cause of that mysterious experience. A loud "Anat!" pierced her right ear before she could utter a word. Felicity was on the other side of the line.

"Yes, Felicity, I shall be in your office in a few minutes. Don't go anywhere!"

Dr. Athenaion sprinted to her car and practically flew through the campus and then through North Street all the way to Murrah High School.

Felicity was pacing the floor when her sister reached the half-open door of her office. They did not greet each other because there was no time or reason for pleasantries and platitudes. They simply sank into each other's arms in a very tight embrace that lasted for several long seconds. Their heaving chests spoke the language of sisterly love, of divine love, the love that gives rise to all types of love.

"What happened?" Dr. Athenaion asked after they had reluctantly extricated themselves from the embrace. Let me look at you first—are you all right?"

"Yes, I am fine—"

"Then, what is it?" Dr. Athenaion asked impatiently, interrupting her sister. "Is it the Principal? Is he going to fire you? Is it Norman?"

"No."

"Then what?"

"Please, Anat, sit!"

Dr. Athenaion sank into the chair opposite Felicity's desk and stared at her sister with frightened eyes and trembling lips. But Felicity could not speak, not immediately, because she was trying to swallow some saliva. Her throat must have been dry, Dr. Athenaion thought. But in truth, that was not the reason for her inability to speak. She looked at her sister with equally frightened eyes and silent lips. "Felicity, I am not a child. I can take bad news—"

"I thought so too, but in this case, it is easier thought or felt than done."

"How bad?

"Bad! I am devastated, Anat!" Tears were slowly welling up in Felicity's eyes, eventually spilling over onto her cheeks. The wracking sobs followed close behind.

"Please, Felicity!"

"He will die," she said, still tearing and sobbing.

"Who will die?" Unable to control herself anymore, Dr. Athenaion abandoned her side of the desk and went to her sister's side. She stroked her back softly.

"My father, our father!" Felicity said.

"Our father?" Dr. Athenaion returned in an unbelieving voice as if to imply, "You must be teasing me! Are you serious? He was fine when we had dinner with him and the whole family last Sunday."

"Yes, but as you know, he never spoke or complained about his problems. He always kept them from us."

"What makes you think that he will die?"

"He has been suffering from kidney infection for about five months. At first, the family physician prescribed a dose of antibiotics. It was helpful for a few weeks, then the infection returned. Another dose of antibiotics, this time stronger, was prescribed. It, too, was helpful for a little more than a month. Then the physician prescribed the strongest antibiotic on the medical market. Its effect did not fare better than the effect of the other treatments."

"But why didn't we know about these infections?" Dr. Athenaion, whose impatience was mounting in her mind and heart, asked, interrupting her sister. "You share your life with our parents."

"Yes, I do, but you should know how they, especially Father, thinks and acts. Frankly, he did not take these infections seriously! Besides, neither he nor Mother wishes to burden us with their problems. They think that the problems we have are more than enough for us!"

"*But their life is our problem*. They are our parents. Their wellbeing and their life are an integral part of ours."

"You have put your finger on the problem."

"What is the problem?"

"They seriously believe that they should not burden us. As you must know, they had always been protective of their children. They have intercepted or undermined any factor that obstructs or interrupts the normal flow of our lives, and they respect our physical and psychological spaces. Unlike so many parents, they do not like to be a nuisance. All they want and all they expect from us is to be successful and happy, nothing else. One day, in a conversation with Mother, she quoted Father saying, 'Didn't you and I chart and steer our lives by our own efforts? Haven't we always prized our privacy and individuality? Why should we infringe on theirs? Didn't we hope from the depth of our mind that they become *human individuals*? Have you forgotten, my dearest, that we both agreed that we love them truly when we see them grow as *human individuals*?' But I tend to think that they respect our individuality because they love us intensely. Even Mother once remarked to me that love alone is the ultimate source of human respect for human individuality and the wellbeing of people. I sometimes think, Anat, that they are bears ready to fight to the death for their cubs—"

"But," Dr. Athenaion interrupted her sister, "we are not cubs anymore, we are adult individuals, we are successful professionally, and we are reasonably happy."

"Yes, they know this, and they are proud of us—"

"If they know this, and they do, they should allow us to love them the way they loved and continue to love us. Love cannot and should not be one-sided. Love is not love if it is not mutual. Didn't Father once say that *we should love gracefully and receive love gracefully*?"

"I tend to think, Anat, that our parents have learned to love but not to receive it."

"What do you mean?"

"Love is not merely an emotion, a reaction, or an attitude we assume toward someone; it is *also* a skill. So many parents love their children, spouses, or friends but do not know *how* to love them. Knowing how to love someone requires practice, patience, trust, tolerance, determination, always acceptance with open arms. This kind of orientation cannot be punitive. It may well be the case, Felicity, that we have been negligent toward our parents. They were never selfish or expedient in their love for us. But they have not practiced the skill, and I should say art, of receiving it. Don't you think *it is our duty to teach them how to practice it*?"

"It may be too late," Felicity said.

"To do what?"

"They did not allow themselves to practice it, and we did not give it to them either. Can they practice it if Father is dying and Mother is getting older and older?"

"It is never too late to do the good, and it is never too late to right a wrong."

"Yes, as a matter of principle, but not in our case. How can Father acquire, or learn, the skill of receiving love if he is dying?"

"Are you sure he is dying?"

"I am sure, but I wish to goodness that I am wrong."

"What makes you think he is dying? Tell me what happened—so far. I promise to remain focused on your answer."

"When Mother discovered that the antibiotic was ineffective, she called Stanley and told him about the infection—when the treatments began and how he was treated. The only response he gave to Mother was, 'I shall be there shortly!' And in fact, he was at home a few minutes later. His face was pale, his eyes restless, and his lips were tremulous. He could not speak. Although pale, his complexion was a living image of apprehension, of anxiety, of fear. He embraced Mother firmly and held her for a long time, then with a feeling of disappointment, said, "Why?"

"'What do you mean, son?'

"'Am I not a physician? Why wasn't I informed of my father's kidney infection? Am I a stranger?'"

"Mother could not speak with her lips, not immediately, but she spoke with her tears, and the tears that flowed from her eyes were tears of confusion, of regret, of pain, and they were a cry for help! It was impossible for her to give Stanley any rational explanation. The only remark she made was, 'Please, be gentle with him. His love for you, your brother, and sisters is infinite. He meant well. He simply did not wish to cumber you. He really thought that the infection could be treated with antibiotics. He never entertained the possibility of cancer or anything like it. I should have called you, my dear. Perhaps I am more guilty than your father.'"

"'Where is Father now?'

"'He should be here any minute.'"

"When did all this happen?" Dr. Athenaion asked, infuriated.

"Yesterday."

"What exactly did happen?"

"When Father arrived, Stanley took him to Dr. Fowler's office, Professor of Urology at the University Medical Center. He X-rayed his kidneys and then did CT scans, as well as ultrasound tests. The images they took showed that malignant cancer has already spread throughout the left kidney."

"Malignant?"

"They also detected a few malignant cells in the right kidney. The next step is to reveal the extent to which the cancer has spread to other parts of the body. But the urologist was not happy about his findings. Stanley is devastated, so is Mother."

"Why was I left out?"

"You were not left out, dearest Anat! Even Kenny was not informed until now. Mother called him. He should be here any second now. The gloom that settled in our home when we discovered this bad news was oppressive, stifling. I was so depressed. I could neither think nor feel anything. I was absolutely numb. I felt like someone had clobbered me on the head with a steel bat. More than once, Mother tried to console me, yet, it was I who should have tried to console her. I cannot express to you the depth of her love for Father and for us."

"And Father? How does he feel?"

"He has been calm, reflective. He behaves the way he always did."

"How did he react to the news that cancer has spread to the other kidney and might have traveled to other parts of his body?"

"He is reluctant to express or, in any way, reveal his feelings or reaction to the radiologist's findings. In the evening, when Stanley asked if he had any questions about the results of the tests he has already had and the ones he will have this afternoon, his response was short and simple. 'I understand Dr. Fowler's analysis of my situation and what I should expect in the coming days, perhaps weeks.' He conducted himself last night the way he did every night as if nothing has disturbed the course of his life, as if no calamity has befallen our family. Whenever Mother or I made a comment on his condition, he smiled and instantly changed the subject. It is clear to me that he does not wish to spend our time, or his, on his illness."

"Why?"

"For the reason I have just mentioned: he does not wish to cumber us. The only thing he wishes is that we carry on with our lives as smoothly as possible. But I think this is going too far."

"Suppose," Dr. Athenaion said, "you, or we as a family, talk about it—what can we say? What can we do? The only thing we can discuss is whether he will have radiation treatment, how long he will live, how much he will suffer, and how to manage his pain. But these are facts. We cannot change them, can we? But although we cannot change them, we can change ourselves."

"How?"

"We can learn to accept his imminent death calmly, and we can learn to live more productively than we have been doing."

"But that will not be easy to do."

"Do you have any other rational suggestion? Would Father wish us to opt for any other choice? Hasn't he always encouraged us to be the individuals we should be, to respect life, and promote it in our lives and the lives of others? Isn't it our duty to *live* as long as we exist? Isn't human life a gift we should prize, enjoy, and cherish—?

"Yes, but—"

"But what?"

"Living with a father who, with our mother, brought us into this world and nourished us biologically and spiritually, who was a constant source of wisdom, who remains an integral part of our lives, a father whose love is an invaluable treasure—yes, living with this kind of father is something and living without him is completely something else. How will we live without such a father? How can we live in the desolate emptiness he will leave behind? This is what troubles me, Anat?"

"Yes, but my dear Felicity, who said that not only this treasure but also all the treasures of the world, including our lives, will last or that we have a right to immortality? Don't you think that we should teach ourselves to live with this painful fact? "How?'

"By understanding it—"

"How?"

"This takes learning and contemplation. We understand it by viewing it, comprehending it, and accepting it as a fact of natural and human existence. This fact is governed by the law of change: nothing remains the same; everything that exists will sooner or later perish. If we acknowledge the supremacy of this law, I mean, if we grasp its meaning truly and recognize it existentially in the way we live, we can see that neither we nor any other type of being is entitled to eternal life. But, if we are not entitled to it, why should we fret or curse the gods when death whispers in our ears, 'Your time is up?' Have people across the past centuries concocted the idea of immortality out of ignorance of this fact? Do the animals rebel against death? I know we are rational animals, but we are integral parts of nature, just like the stone, the river, and the wind. Is the demand, even the desire, for immortality symptomatic of a moral cancer the ancient Greeks called *hubris*? Is it fear of the unknown, of non-being?"

"But this desire seems to be inherent in human nature," Felicity responded. "It is expressed in most, if not all, the literary works of the ancient and modern worlds."

"Not really! It is expressed by those who are enamored of themselves, especially the people who are hungry for power, pleasure, and glory. A large number of people, especially those who are close to the earth, such as farmers, tend to recognize their mortality and accept it with a deep sense of humility. 'Nothing endures' is a generally recognized piece of wisdom in all the cultures of the world."

"Some people would argue that they deserve immortality primarily because they love life at the human level. *Human life* is intrinsically good. It is justifiable to desire the good and do it. Therefore, since life is a supreme good, since it is always good to seek life as a permanent possession, it is justifiable to desire immortal life."

"Desiring life as a permanent possession and desiring immortality are two different types of desire. People who love human life and treat it as a supreme good may desire a *long life* but *not eternal life*—"

"Why?"

"Because such people also know, or should know, that change is king. If nothing changes, if everything remains the same, life will not exist. We should always remember that life is a dynamic phenomenon: it is an emanation of the on-going process of the cosmic process, regardless of its type or degree. If this process stops, life ceases to exist. Accordingly, if human life is a process of growth and development, that is, if it is a process, if the essence of this process is valuable achievements in the areas of social, political, intellectual, religious scientific, and moral experience, if change is a necessary condition of this kind of life, human beings should not regret or curse the gods when it is time for them to leave this world. On the contrary, they should light a candle of gratitude to the gods for allowing them to participate in the rite of human living—"

The phone rang in the middle of the conversation. Kenny was on the other side of the line: "We have been waiting for you for quite a while, Felicity. Are you all right? Mother is worried about you!"

"I am fine, Kenny!"

"And Anat? We have been calling her at the office, but she does not seem to be there."

"She is not there because she is with me. We are both fine. We should be home in a few minutes."

"Sorry, Anat!" Felicity said as she was replacing the handset. "I am the cause of the delay. I should not have asked you so many questions. I do not know what happened to me. I felt like a flurry of questions was swarming my mind demanding immediate answers. I could not resist them. Perhaps this is not the right time to ask them because I know that the entire family must be waiting for us."

"But it is right to ask them," Dr. Athenaion emphasized as they were walking toward their cars in the school's parking lot. "Death is uppermost on our minds, particularly Father's." The sisters delayed a few more minutes in the parking lot.

"Why did you single out, Father?"

"Because self-composure does not mean or, as you pointed out earlier, does not necessarily imply frigidity of the heart, emotions, or feelings; it only implies being in command of one's heart, emotions, and feelings. A volcano can be raging in your heart, and yet you can control its flames and sparks. I tend to think that our father's heart is currently such a volcano."

"What makes you say that?"

"Love is a flame of fire. When a loving father like ours knows how he will die, when this love has been the main source of his happiness, indeed his reason for being, don't you think that this flame will explode into a volcano at the realization that his death is around the corner?"

"Anat!" Felicity said in the most serene voice you can imagine. "You must be a spy!"

"A spy?"

"*A spy of the human heart*!"

"I wish my dear Felicity."

Two glasses of wine were waiting for the sisters when they arrived at home. The Athenaions always shared a glass of wine when they visited as a family. "A family visit," Henry once said, "is a moment of celebration!"

That afternoon was not an exception. One glass of wine was waiting for Dr. Athenaion on one side of the coffee table, and another glass was waiting for Felicity on the other side. "You must have had a hard day. I was worried about you," Dora said when the two sisters sat in their chairs.

"Yes, Mother, it was a long and hard day for me, as well as for Felicity. This happens once in a while," Dr. Athenaion said and raised her glass a little, "I propose a toast in honor of Stanley's inquiry into the ontic basis of human nature!"

"I second the proposal," Henry responded and added, "he will be able to unlock the secret of self-consciousness. This is my wish!"

"It is mine, Father," Stanley said as he took a sip of wine.

"It seems to me that deciphering this mystery," Dr. Athenaion, added, "is one of the most valuable gifts to humankind, no less valuable than that of discovering fire, electricity, the wheel, or the theory of evolution. Discovering the code of self-consciousness is supremely valuable, but whether I shall accomplish this feat is a farfetched expectation. I am an ordinary researcher trying to advance our knowledge of the source and dynamics of self-consciousness."

"All researchers are ordinary people until they complete their research, and they are extraordinary when their accomplishments are extraordinary. Unlocking the secret of self-consciousness is not an ordinary accomplishment," Dr. Athenaion said.

"I fully agree with Anat," Henry seconded his daughter.

"Although it is sometimes possible to disagree with Stanley, it is always impossible to disagree with Anat!"

"Yes," Stanley said, "that is why she should be the neuroscientist conducting, or at least steering, the project I am working on."

"Are you speaking as a scientist or as my dear brother?"

"As a scientist and as your dear brother."

"Oh, Anat! You should be in my place," Stanley retorted.

"If she is, she will miss the philosophy that thrives in her mind," Henry remarked.

"Dinner will be served in a few minutes," Dora announced.

Kenny, who was waiting for the right moment to change the subject of the conversation, asked Stanley about Dr. Fowler's estimate of his father's tests. He knew that the conversation, which was initiated and indirectly steered by his father, was intended to avoid any discussion of his medical tests. Still, he could not comply with his father's wish. "Malignant cancer has spread in the left kidney," Stanley said, "and has begun to spread in the right kidney. It must be an aggressive kind of cancer. Tomorrow we shall do more tests to determine whether it has spread to other glands and hopefully ascertain the best way to treat it. But Dr. Fowler is not pleased with his findings so far."

Dora, who was doing her best to control her tears and sobs, left the living room and went to the kitchen. She let loose those tears and sobs as she stood at the sink and stared into the infinite space on the other side of the window without knowing what she was doing. She wept and sobbed and sighed abundantly. Softly, almost imperceptibly, Felicity went and stood next to her. She too wept and sobbed. They remained silent for a few moments, dried their eyes, and silently moved the pots to the dining room.

"Dinner is served," Felicity announced after she and her mother placed the pots, plates, and silverware on the dining room table.

Dr. Athenaion was no less emotional, no less distressed, and no less agitated than her mother and sister, but, unlike them and more like her father, she was able to control her emotions and assume an attitude of self-composure. She stared at her father's face for a few long seconds soon after he sat at the head of the table, as he always did, and then raised her wine glass and said, "My father and my mother deserve the highest honor, admiration, and respect in my life. This seat," she said, and looking at Henry's chair, continued, "is holy and shall always be holy. It is holy because it was consecrated by your love for me, my sister, and my brothers. We are fortunate to be your children, Father, and you too, Mother!!"

Although no one noticed it, a tear left the corner of her right eye as she gulped a sip of wine from her glass.

"To our Father and Mother!" The brothers and sisters cheered in unison.

Unlike any other dinner they had shared lately, the Athenaions ate their supper in silence. Dora was deeply concerned about her husband, so were her children. Frankly, the image of their father leaving them forever was quaking the peace of their minds and hearts. They could not hide their feelings and anxieties. How can anyone hide them if they know that their beloved father is slowly slipping into the infinite world of non-being? Experiencing this kind of slippage is different from thinking about it, philosophically, psychologically, or socially. In this kind of experience, you do not only feel the process of slipping, but you also witness it, you feel it, and you feel the seams of your relationship, your bond, with the person you love crackling and splintering into bits of nothing! It is like pulling out a beautiful, fruit-bearing tree from its roots. The life that used to radiate from its leaves and branches, and the life that awaits you when you eat its fruits, slowly fades away, leaving a dead tree behind! Loving people tend to have this kind of experience when they witness the gradual transition of the people they love from this world into the world of nothing. But, you do not only witness this slipping as a spectacle taking place before your eyes, but you also experience it taking place within you because in losing the person you love, you lose a part of yourself! This kind of experience is devastating.

That was an excruciatingly painful and troubling visit for Henry and his family. But his mind was big, and his heart bigger than his mind. He felt the tension that was reverberating wildly in the dining room, and he understood both its meaning and its source. When everyone was about to finish their supper, he spoke:

"Neither you nor I can conceal, suppress, or ignore your concern and sorrow for me. It is, I think, wrong and harmful to everyone's sanity and general wellbeing to indulge in this kind of concealment or suppression. On the contrary, it is the duty of rational beings to be true and honest to the facts of human life, and it is their duty to be realistic especially in the critical moments of their lives—would you agree with me Anat, Stanley, Kenny, Felicity, and you the jewel of my life?" The children nodded softly, but the jewel of his life allowed tears to glide over her cheeks with a wild, yet tender, stare into her husband's face. "Tomorrow Stanley will supervise the second phase of the tests on the state of my cancer. I shall submit to their results. Their purpose is to confirm what we already know. But I have a feeling, as you do, that it will be difficult, and practically impossible, to stop the spread of the cancer or to eliminate it from my body. Only a miracle can save me from the deadly claws of this cancer. But we do not live in the age of miracles. Ask Stanley. He knows."

"You are agonizing over my impending departure from this world. The sparks of this agony are clashing violently in the air, and in the silence, of this room. They are clashing equally violently in every fiber of my being because they spring from your loving hearts. I hear these clashes, and I feel the sting of their sparks. Although they are dear to me because they originate from your hearts, they torment me for the same reason. I am not a heartless husband and father. But when the power that governs the world created me, it created a flaming heart."

"For some strange reason, I have been living from, and with, the fact that my death is an *imminent possibility*, not in the sense that I would be dead in one hour or day or month or when I reach the age of seventy, not in the sense that I would be dead any moment, and not in the sense that some god has whispered the time of my death in my ear, no, *but in the sense that it is inherent in the very process of living,* of existing. It is the nature of things, material, and human that their being or existence and living is permeated with *non-being*. Non-being is an essential ingredient of their being. If you remove the element of non-being, you also remove the element of being, which is tantamount to their annihilation. It may strike you as strange, perhaps unbelievable, that the same applies to non-being, it is i*nconceivable* apart from being. We cannot speak of non-being, and we cannot use terms such as 'not,' 'no,' or any other mode of negation without simultaneously thinking of being. This strange, but logical, relationship between being and non-being is not a theoretical, or merely conceptual, relation, but ontological in its very essence. It is a fact, and this fact is the constitutive structure of our being and life."

"These two elements, being and non-being, are fused in the phenomenon of life. The relation between them is dialectical." Henry's eyes were focused on Dr. Athenaion's face when he was expounding this rather intricate concept. "The life of the human being who acts on the stage of human history is a synthesis of these elements. I cannot explain this synthesis through Aristotelian logic. Still, I can say that the outcome, or result, of this process, is the different types of being, and consequently, the various objects that constitute the fabric of the material and human worlds. But I am convinced that this relation is the essence of every existing object, regardless of its type of value in this vast universe. I tend to think that it is the impetus of the life we feel, whose primary drive is survival at the biological and human levels, the pulse of life that reverberates in our minds and hearts when we pursue worthwhile goals and when we accomplish the various tasks of daily living. It is also the essence of the enthusiasm that underlies the designs and implementation of our life-projects. Yes, this most basic enthusiasm for life originates from this dynamic relationship between being and non-being. Whenever either one of them advances, the other counteracts it. For example, don't you feel bored when you realize a meaningless goal? Your drive to undergo meaningful activity is a drive for being. We cease to exist as the human beings we are when we stop our pursuit of meaningful goals."

"Now, when I say that I am living from and with the imminent possibility of my death and that this possibility is inherent to the structure of my inner self as a human being, I mean that I proceed in my attempt to understand the meaning of existence in general and my own existence in particular, from a reasoned, firm, and clear recognition of the fact that every moment of my life, sad or happy, successful or failure, boring or creative, great or mediocre, peaceful or troublesome, carries within its womb the possibility of my non-being, the fact that my life is temporary, and more importantly, that it is a gift. The 'I' that presides over the activities of my mind and heart contains the element of non-being as one of its essential structures. It is always important to remind ourselves that we begin to die the moment we are born and that the final target of change is perishing."

"This recognition is and should be, the most significant factor in the design and implementation of our life-projects. It awakens in us the consciousness of the meaning of human life, 'Why do I exist?' How should I live if my existence is temporary? This consciousness emerges when we first experience the human importance of meaning: human satisfaction, joy, delight, and jubilation, in short, zest for life. It expands in depth and richness, the more we grow in the different areas of experience. This kind of experience, which we crave in everything we do, generates in us a profound appreciation of life. This appreciation is founded in the structure of the capacity for value experiences: aesthetic, moral, religious, intellectual, social, practical, and political experiences. A value experience is essentially an experience of meaning. Our desire for the experience of meaning is inherent in human nature, and we can say that that it is the strongest desire we feel in the pursuit of the different goals in our lives. Do we desire the objects we seek in our individual lives if we do not deem them good or, in some way, important? Don't we, by nature, seek pleasure and avoid pain? The point I would like to underscore is that the enjoyment of meaning is not only the most essential fruit of human life but also its reason for being. Therefore, it is the crown of human life. Don't some people commit suicide or lose themselves to drugs, alcohol, or other types of orgiastic experiences when, for some reason, they discover that their life is spiritually empty or meaningless?"

"When we discover, or recognize, the absolute value of human life, that it is intrinsically valuable, we cannot but listen to the voice of time whispering in our ears that our lives are temporary and that it is our duty to maximize the enjoyment of the meaning we deserve and for which we exist. We also hear that it is sinful to waste it. We can articulate this twofold whisper in the following way: 'Be careful! Make sure that you do not waste your time. Your life is valuable, but it is short. What makes your existence dramatic, and some would say tragic is that you live once. You do not only live as a flicker in the cosmic process, but you are also a drop of time. Therefore, wasting it is tantamount to wasting yourself. But you are a sacred drop of time, so is your life. Accordingly, it is wrong to waste any minute of it. Always remember that the building blocks of your life are the events in which you construct your action and consequently your life."

"Those two modes of consciousness, that you are temporary and that your life is absolutely valuable, do not only imply but necessarily provoke the question, 'How should I live?' 'How can I fulfill the purpose for which I exist?' This is not a simple question, but as my dear Anat explained in some detail in an earlier conversation, exceedingly complicated. This question is not the luxury of the intellectual, and it is not theoretical or abstract. It arises from an existential encounter with the most radical predicament of human consciousness, and it is such a predicament because, unlike plants and animals, human beings confront themselves as a problem to themselves. They are not only bodies, but they are also minds, hearts, and wills. They are not given to the world, as Anat has taught me, as readymade realities but as realities to be made, and to be made by the individual and no one else. How? How can they live according to the essence that exists in them as a potentiality awaiting realization? Put differently, how can they live as human individuals? But this is not all. How should they live as individuals in an unfriendly nature and a short period? The voice that issues from the human essence the moment human consciousness opens up its eyes to the world, that is, the moment reason emerges from the womb of adolescence, whispers in its ears: 'You have about fifty to eighty years to live, assuming that you are not struck down with a fatal illness, or are involved in a crushing accident during your youth. In this short time, you must give birth to yourself as a human individual, after which you are expected to conduct yourself as an individual, and then you will transit into the world of oblivion. This is your destiny. But, then, this very voice adds, 'You and no one else has all the resources you need to chart and realize your destiny by your wisdom and by the sweat of your brow. Therefore, you are responsible for the kind of person you will be and the kind of life you will lead. When your time is up, you will stand before the bench of your conscience. You will be the judge, the jury, and the executioner of your judgment. You may feel proud of yourself, of the life you designed, and the way you have implemented it. If you are proud of your life, joy will be the master of your heart, and peace will be the master of your mind when you leave this world. But if you are ashamed of it, guilt will be the master of your mind and heart, and you will leave the world trembling with fear and shame. Alone you came into the world, and alone you will leave it."

"What I have just said is based on my experience and reflection on the meaning of human existence. You can treat it as a personal testament, not as a generalization or as a neatly philosophical statement. The point that merits our special attention is that listening to the voice of time and contemplating the fact that death is an imminent possibility inherent in our very being should be treated as a call not only to take our lives seriously but especially to live it authentically, that is, according to the values that reflect the essential demands of human nature. How do we know them? Anat should answer this question. But a remark based on my personal experience is in order. I make it only because I feel a strong desire to empty my human self to the family I loved affectionately and devotedly all my life, and I wish to present this self as a gift before I depart this world."

"We may say, as Anat has argued more than once, that we live authentically when we meet our basic human needs according to the values and beliefs which have guided and sustained the progress of human civilization since its inception. Implied in this premise is that the life we live should originate from our minds and wills. But these beliefs and values exist as ideals, general ideas, as schemas. The recalcitrant question authentic people face in pursuing their life-projects is, 'How do we act according to these beliefs and values? How do we translate the essence of a moral value into a particular judgment in this particular situation?' No two human beings think, feel, value, and respond to the problems they face in the same way. There are no formulated rules for acting according to these beliefs and values, primarily because the circumstances of human life are constantly changing and because human beings are, to some extent individual, unique. There are general guidelines for aesthetic, scientific, and moral behavior in the different practical and professional fields, but they are not universal prescriptions or judgments. Past experience, both individual and social, is always a rich source of insight—of how we should act. Still, it cannot deliver a finally articulated judgment on how we should act in a particular situation. As you can see, it is not enough to explore the logical or theoretical structure of the beliefs and values we should act on. It is crucially important to explore how to act according to them, that is, how to develop the art of acting on them."

"Although I planned and tried to lead my life based on this vital truth of human existence, I do not know whether I succeeded in my attempt. All I can say is that I made this attempt with all my will, unwaveringly. It is difficult for people to judge their life objectively and adequately. But it does not matter whether I did or did not succeed, first, because one of my feet is already in the land of death and, second, because, at present, I feel inner peace and harmony. My sojourn with you will be short, but it will be an eternity of happiness for me, and I hope for you. Many people aim at longevity as their primary concern in this world. However, it is wise to aim at the good, the kind of good that promotes the wellbeing of others, that advances their intellectual, emotional, moral, aesthetic, material, and social wellbeing. Those who pursue this aim and succeed in realizing it in their individual lives frown upon longevity. What is the use of living a long, very long, but a miserable, lonely, or unproductive life? But choosing a good life rather than a long one is not a matter of wagering between them, but is instead founded in the nature of existence in general and human existence in particular. Just as the apple tree exists to give apples and just as apples nourish human beings biologically, so human beliefs and values exist to nourish our minds and hearts. However, frowning upon longevity does not necessarily imply shunning it. No, it only implies that it is not the supreme good of human life. On the contrary, it is our duty to desire a long life, *while recognizing that,* regardless of its length, it will be temporary."

"Nevertheless, although the remaining stretch of my life will be brief, I experience a profound feeling of gratitude. I did not have an interview with the power that created me, I did not discuss the desirability of my existence with it, and I was not allowed to reflect on the matter. Yet, I know in the depth of mind that such a power exists and that it has been the architect of this amazing cosmos. There is no reason for me to establish the validity of this claim, at least not now, and there is no reason for me to have an audience with the power that created me, although I stood in its luminous presence more than once during my lifetime. It is trifling whether it has a particular essence or shape. What matters to me as a recipient of this infinitely valuable gift, the gift of celebrating the rite of life, is that I feel a personal relationship with this power not only in my own life but also in the scheme of nature and, especially, in the history of human civilization. No cultivated mind that stands before the intricacy of the human and natural orders, and who ponders the mystery that permeates them the way the light of the sun permeates the space of the solar system that feels its living pulse, that drinks a cup of its nectar with every dawn, can fail to see its presence, its radiance, its warmth, and most of all its wisdom. It strikes me as strange, indeed outlandish, that many people believe in the wisdom of the scientist, the philosopher, and the sage, but not in the luminous wisdom of the power that underlies this amazing universe. Could it be that they accept this kind of wisdom because it is the only one they know? What if some power opened a new window in their minds that overlooks a new dimension of being that they have never seen before by their ordinary means of knowing? What then? What if such a power already exists in their minds? It is insignificant whether this power hears what I am now saying, whether it speaks Fenech or Khalkha, or any kind of language, or a being that possesses any human qualities or powers. How can I, Henry Athenaion, this ripple that will soon pass into the realm of non-being, this frail, negligible emergent in the cosmic process—yes, how can this ripple that made the confession of his life before his beloved wife and children understand the meaning of wisdom, seek it, and value it above everything as the royal road to human growth and development, while treating it as the highest intellectual value if the power that made my existence possible is not infinitely wiser than any human being? How can I love and seek wisdom if its possibility is not inherent in the structure of the cosmic process?

"The feeling of gratitude I experience for being a beneficiary of the gift of life is rooted in this intimate relationship I have with the Creator of the universe. Since I am a witness to its inner working in the cosmos and in my life, how can I falsify or betray the truth of this witness? What may appear to you as strange, and perhaps as mysterious, is that the feeling of gratitude I experience is not merely a feeling. It is also an attitude, a posture of mind, and as such, an integral part of my mind and heart. It underlies the way I have been thinking, feeling, and acting in my personal, family, and public life. This kind of gratitude is not a kind of *quid pro quo*, something for something, which is characteristic of business, social, and legal relations, but a recognition of goodness; it *reflects an ontological recognition* of the ultimate."

"Do truly loving parents expect a 'thank you' from their children for giving birth to them, enabling them to stand on their feet as individuals, and planting the seeds of knowledge, love, and happiness in their minds? Do true friends say, or have to say, 'thank you' for good deeds they perform for each other? Regardless of how it appears in our lives, goodness as a value is not quantifiable. The only reward a person should expect from performing a good deed is the pleasure, indeed honor, of being allowed to do good! Doing good always denotes a moment of human growth and development. The growth we experience when doing good to others induces reciprocal growth in our humanity. Can the joy parents feel when they see their children flourishing morally, socially, professionally, and as citizens, be measured in terms of money, praise, or any kind of reward? Isn't the person who spends weeks on end in the hospital next to the bed of a sick friend, willing to sacrifice everything they own infinitely happier than the person who drinks a few cups of pleasure every day? Don't artists feel the most profound satisfaction in their lives when they know that the work they have created is good or aesthetically beautiful? The monetary value of the artwork, as the history of art and creation clearly shows, is independent of its aesthetic or human value."

"But I am not only grateful to the power that made my existence possible and granted me the opportunity to participate in the ritual of human living, I am also equally grateful for your presence in my life. The medium in and through which I have been celebrating this ritual of human living during my adult life has been my family—my wife, who is the love of my life, and my children who are the fruits of this love. I am the person you now see because of you. I am a husband, a father, and a teacher. Aren't these roles and dimensions of my life, the source, and the basis of my identity? But again, could I have been a husband without my wife, without her love and devotion to her family? Could I have been a father without you, my loving and admirable children? Could I have performed the function of a teacher without my family? These three functions are organically interrelated. The individual I am is a synthesis of these three functions. The inner peace, which defines the essence of my happiness, originates from the activity of performing these functions. Again, could I have been able to contemplate the history of civilization and the mystery that infuses the universe, and could I have felt the warmth of the divine without being the individual that I am? I do not exaggerate if I say that the gratitude I feel toward my family, to every one of you, is a concrete embodiment of the gratitude I feel toward the power that created me. I frequently felt that this warmth enlivened my mind and was a shining ray of that power. Some people look for it in some transcendent realm while others wait until they die in the hope that they will see and feel it in Heaven. They may be justified in their looking and waiting. But I feel that this light, which is the source of the universe, permeates the universe and makes it a profoundly luminous presence for the human mind and heart. Those who have a desire to witness it and live from it are, at present, few. I say 'few' because it takes desire, will, time, devotion, and contemplation, as well as a life devoted to goodness, to move closer to it. Not many people are willing or ready to seek The Light, not because they are unable to but because the conditions of seeking it are not available to them. These conditions are summoned by genuine education, the kind that enables the individual to raise the ultimate question of the meaning and reason for being human, that opens up the fountain of love in their hearts and imbues their wills with the necessary courage to seek the good, the true, and the beautiful."

"People who meet these conditions can easily see that, although they are necessary conditions for the pursuit of happiness, knowledge, pleasure, and social recognition, they are not singly or even collectively the purpose of human existence. These conditions derive their value from the fact that they are essential for the achievement of happiness. Can people be truly happy if they are ignorant, poor, or oppressed? Our purpose as human beings is to grow in our humanity, in the experience and appreciation of goodness, beauty, and wisdom."

"I know that some of the ideas I communicated to you in the preceding remarks are vague, some controversial, and some in need of development of validation. I hope you will allow me to clarify or defend them during the following weeks. I was anxious to communicate them now only because I am afraid that the cancer will be spreading exceedingly rapidly from now on. So, it might constrict the normal functioning of my mental powers."

"I shall conclude these remarks with a request, one you should not decline but take seriously. I make it with a special accent to my wife, to the woman who stole my heart the moment my eyes settled on her sublime countenance, to the woman who stood by my side and never left me during the good and bad times alike, to the woman who accepted me with my weaknesses, strengths, and idiosyncrasies, to the woman who nourished my children and sucked the milk of life from her love. She has always been the source of the warmth and inspiration I needed to be the individual I am. If death means losing the breath of our life, I can assure you that my death will be losing the light of my life. The source of this light was my wife—"

Dora, who was listening to Henry's confession with tears in her eyes and sobs stuck in her throat, could not control them anymore. They gushed out from her inner being as the most moving torrent of human love you can conceive! Her sadness was so intense, so profound, so moving, she could not listen to the rest of her husband's confession. She left the room. Felicity rose to her feet and was about to follow her mother to the kitchen, but her father stopped her. "Let me be with her, my dear," he mumbled and kissed his daughter on the head.

Reverent silence prevailed in the dining room when Henry had left to join his wife. No one of the children expected this confession, and no one comprehended, not immediately, its significance. They looked at each other with curious, baffled eyes. It is strange, and sometimes puzzling, how some people, regardless of the level of their intellectual, emotional, moral, and social development, can often not see, much less understand, the people with whom they lived much of their lives, be they husbands, wives, children, co-workers, or colleagues. "I never dreamed that my father is a volcano of love!" Felicity said.

"Family love, yes, but romantic love?" Kenny retorted.

"Family, human, even romantic love originates from one source—divine love," Dr. Athenaion said. "Love is a *dynamis*; it is a spirit that aims at a union with the other. Isn't love of friendship a bond of union with the friend, divine love a bond of union with God, or family love a bond of union between the members of the family? But when the dimension of love is not only romantic but also human, as it is with our parents, when it is sanctified by the hand of God, it becomes a flame of fire. Our parents have been living in, and from this kind of love from the moment they first met to this day."

"I tend to think that we do our best to remain the shining torches they kindled in our minds and hearts." She paused for a few seconds, then added reflectively, "I propose that beginning tomorrow, we do our best to share our evening meal with our parents daily. You can invite Norman to these meals, dear Felicity, and you too, Kenny, can invite Maggie to them. I hope they know that they are members of the family. We simply cannot leave our parents alone during this critical period of their lives. What I have just said is not a dictation, only a proposal, one that comes more from the heart than the mind."

"It is an excellent proposal," Stanley said.

"I agree with you, Stanley," Kenny seconded his brother.

Felicity left her chair and embraced her sister, warmly. She left a few tears on her head. They, too, were warm.

CHAPTER FOUR

Another Duel between Dr. Athenaion and the God of Death

When Dr. Athenaion opened the door of her apartment after she visited with her family that evening, all the lights, even the light of her bedroom, were on. Startled, she froze at the threshold. She knew without a shred of doubt that she had turned them off when she left for office that morning. The only person who could have turned them on was Felicity, for she had a key to the apartment, but she was with her sister in the afternoon. Therefore, an intruder must have broken and was perhaps lying in wait for her somewhere in the apartment. The mere thought of this possibility, which flashed through her consciousness as she was standing at the threshold of the door, filled her with fear, mostly fear of the unknown because she did not know whether the intruder was a burglar, a rapist, a frustrated student, or a pathological killer. This feeling intensified when she suddenly noticed that the lock of the door, as well as those of the windows on the right side of the apartment, were intact, untouched. This situation was a first in her life. She hesitated for a few moments because she could not proceed further into the apartment, for she was not prepared to face a dangerous intruder, and she could not close the door, for she was not sure what the intruder might do. The only viable option left to her was to call Security. But she did not do this either, because the instant she had pulled her phone out of her briefcase she heard a voice. "There is no need to call Security. You are not in danger. No one is going to harm you. Please, come in, Dr. Athenaion. I have been waiting for you! The feeling of fear that gripped her moments ago was transformed into pure rage. She did not expect to meet Mowt again, not at this juncture of her life. The thought of Mowt sitting on the sofa in her living room sent a strong whiff of nausea into her nostrils. She walked toward the living room. "I am not interested in your money or any of your possessions," Mowt continued, "I am interested in your ideas and nothing else."

"What right do you have to intrude in my apartment? How did you break in—" Dr, Athenaion said with palpable anger in her voice.

"I did not break into your apartment. I did not have to! Walls or any physical barrier do not exist for me. I move freely through any mode of space and time. Neither mountains, doors, walls, or solid objects exist for me. Similarly, your rights, regardless of whether they are natural or human, do not apply to me. These are human creations, but I am not a human being. I am Mowt, the God of Death—"

"Stop this nonsense!" Dr. Athenaion snapped, interrupting Mowt.

"What do you mean?"

"What you say is illogical, against common sense, against any type of scientific thinking. No one, not you or any of your gods, can bend these rules. They are the foundation of any type of meaningful discourse. Without them, we would not be having this spat. Therefore, you would not be here without them."

"But these rules do not apply to me. They are only a means of communicating with human beings. Let me remind you of what you seem to have forgotten. I can appear and disappear, and I can assume any form or identity I choose, at any time or place. How can you explain this kind of phenomenon with your logic? Would you like me to disappear from your presence and instantly appear in the form of the man you loved but abandoned you for a Hollywood actress? You still love him and still wish he returns to you by some miracle but as an honest and devoted lover, just like your father! Another woman would have dumped him and looked for another man, but not you, the most honorable woman I have met among human beings! I have a sneaky feeling that you have not forgotten a single word of our conversation but that you've decided not to take me seriously and have, therefore, dismissed me completely from your consciousness. If this is the case, I beg you to take me and what I say seriously!"

This revelation, which was true, magnified the anger that was raging in Dr. Athenaion's heart. "Who is this creature? Am I imagining this encounter? Is he real? If he is," she wondered, "how? How does he know about my love affair and how I feel about Dimitri?" But her doubt was obstructed by the voice of the intruder.

"Please, Dr. Athenaion, do not allow your mind to be burdened by any type or shade of skepticism. It is wise to take me seriously." But Dr. Athenaion was neither interested nor heedful of this or any kind of wisdom coming from the mouth of this creature, perhaps phantom. She was overwhelmed by his inexplicable presence. She simply fixed her eyes on his face, but to her shock, she did not see the intruder. She saw Dimitri, the same man she'd loved ten years earlier. He was as handsome as he was when they were in love with each other, and he was looking at her with the most alluring smile dancing merrily on his lips. Instead of contemplating that face or appreciate that smile, Dr. Athenaion was seized by a feeling of terror. Her lips trembled, and her eyes froze in their sockets. Although her eyes were fixed on him, she did not see the man sitting on the sofa facing her, not because she did not see that beautiful face but because she could not believe what she was seeing. Mowt noticed her state of confusion. "I miss you, Anat!" the lips of that beautiful face said and was at once metamorphosed back into the figure of the Mowt.

"How can you explain this act of metamorphosis? Can you doubt what you have just witnessed and heard?" Mowt asked.

"I do not doubt what I have witnessed and heard, and yet, I cannot believe that you have supernatural powers, that you are the God of Death, or that you even exist—"

"What you say," Mowt said, interrupting Dr. Athenaion, "applies to human beings, but I am not a human being, I am the God of Death, nephew of the Devil, the God of Perishing. I am not in charge of the passing away of people. That is my uncle's function. I oversee human death, the death of people as human beings. Natural existence is the supreme enemy of my uncle, human existence is my supreme enemy. The event in which the human body loses its life, that is, when it ceases to exist, is not real death. It is an event of perishing, of passing from the state of being into the state of non-being. This type of event is peculiar to natural objects. Death is a *human phenomenon,* and as such, that which dies is not physical but *human* in character. When the body perishes, the human dimension of the person ceases to exist because, as your brother argued, the human dimension is centered in the brain."

"But what many people do not seem to realize is that people suffer two types of death, physical and human. Most of them do not pay attention to this fact because material survival is uppermost on their minds, thanks to me. Did you know that many people die at the human level before they are born? What is worse, is that many of them do not possess adequate knowledge of their humanity, much less of the need to grow in it. My aim is to combat and impede their growth in humanity, but that villain, the God of Love, seems to succeed in making it grow in the souls of a few of them."

"How do you achieve this aim? If your uncle is in charge of perishing, if you are in charge of impeding the growth of humanity, how do you practice the obstruction of its growth and development? What exactly do you seek to obstruct or destroy? How can that which is human be destroyed?"

"I aim to destroy what you aim to construct as a teacher, scholar, and citizen. I do not destroy humanity the way my uncle destroys material objects or the way people destroy tables and houses. I destroy humanity by suffocating, or frustrating, the growth of the seeds that give rise to it. When you prevent a seed from sprouting, from realizing the essence that exists in it as a potentiality, you practically undermine its growth and development. Therefore, you should not worry about your life. This does not necessarily imply that I cannot use your body to achieve my aim. I aim at the humanity you seek to plant and nourish in your life and the lives of others and now in the project on the construction of a human community governed by technocrats. What you seek to achieve in working on his project is to create a seed that may grow and become a lighthouse of humanity. I aim to destroy the lighthouse before it is constructed. Its light is an anathema to my mind!"

"In my endeavor to accomplish my aim as Mowt, I always begin with the roots. As you know, the roots of a plant are its foundation. They are the source of the nutrients that make it grow. When the soil in which the plant grows loses the necessary chemicals for its growth, the tree slowly withers away. A human being is like a plant. Nature provides the elements required for the survival of the body. These nutrients are chemicals. When the body does not receive them, primarily, through water, food, and air, the body will wither away—"

"And humanity?" Dr. Athenaion intervened in the way a debater usually intervenes in a heated conversation.

"Here comes the rub! The soil in which humanity is founded and from which it grows is *human community.* Human values, the same values you and your father discussed this evening, are the foundation of human community. The ultimate aim of this community is the cultivation and promotion of human individuality. Your project is an inquiry into the conditions under which human individuality grows and flourishes. Many philosophers have written about this subject, but their ideas are shallow and ineffective. But yours, Dr. Athenaion, are not only genuine, they are also the most constructive, most revolutionary ideas ever conceived by a thinker in the history of human civilization."

"I cannot allow you to develop your ideas into a plan of action. This kind of plan is truly a project of love, and love is my arch enemy. I have been targeting such plans ever since I was created."

"What makes this project of yours extra dangerous is that you are developing it at the wrong turn of the history of civilization—"

"Why?"

"Because I have, so far, succeeded in supporting the growth of a society governed by greedy, ruthless, power-hungry technocrats, not humane technocrats. This type of leadership is indifferent to human values. They allow people to pursue them only because their development is conducive to their own interests. But anyone who infringes or in any way undermines their policies will not last long. I am the power who inspired their type of leadership, and I am the power that will protect them from any forces that may counteract their form of technocracy."

"How?"

"The recent advancement of technology has given rise to a new type of power. In the past, the kings, princes, sultans, or presidents that governed the different societies of the world imposed their will, which was mostly embodied in the laws they enforced through physical force—by physical liquidation, imprisonment, hanging, banishment, or torture. Recent technology has not only changed the identity of those leaders but also how they govern society. They do represent the will of God, reason, the common good, or the highest good of humanity anymore. They do not represent the interests of the people, and they do not represent the spirit of tradition. What is ironic is that governors cannot even be dictators. They represent the interests of the economically powerful class. The type of power that currently governs the world is not religious, military, or ideological, and it is certainly not the power of wisdom; oh, no, it is economic power. Politics is the handmaid of the economically rich. Have you noticed that the traditional monarchs in Europe, the Middle East, and Africa have become businesses? Human institutions such as churches, universities, families, medical clinics, hospitals, book publishers, and science research centers. Why? They have become, thanks to my valiant and successful efforts, businesses. Can anyone of these institutions survive if they are not profitable or materially self-sufficient or marketable? The doctrine I have been spreading for more than two centuries is that money, not God, not Reason, not human values, moves the world. Money is the new god! If you are rich, you are viewed, at least in your lifetime, as wise, good, powerful, happy, and worthy of respect, even if you happen to be a rotten egg morally and intellectually, even if you are miserable or the nastiest creature on the face of the earth! I readily admit that there are many die-hard champions of human values like you, and I have a strong feeling that they will be with us the way the poor will always be with us. Idealists exist because poor, ignorant, hungry, sick, oppressed, and disenfranchised people exist. Notice what happens when some epidemic spreads and threaten the life of society—what is the government's first and immediate response? Save the economy, not the life of the masses! Why? Because if you save the life of the masses, you save the economy. The rich will lose their power without the labor of the masses. You see, I know the value of the stomach! This organ is more important than the heart or the brain you have been emphasizing all your life. People do not care about their minds or hearts, they want a satisfied stomach. The main objective of the capitalist is to keep the stomach of the masses satisfied. They give morsels of freedom, justice, peace, and security to make them feel happy or autonomous." Dr. Athenaion was frowning when Mowt was expounding his general ideas and diagnosis of the human condition. However, Mowt was all too aware of her feelings and inner reaction to what he was saying.

"There is no reason for you to be surprised, Dr. Athenaion, or even outraged, by my understanding of human nature and the dynamics that underlie human action in general. All the institutions of your society carry the banner of human values, as I have just mentioned, only because it is beautiful and fanciful. All your leaders wear the robe of human values, and all of them justify their existence, their goals, and their policies in the name of these values. But, please, don't be deceived by what you see. Hypocrisy, which is supposed to be a great evil, has become a virtue and, more importantly, a way of life. You are an anomaly, Dr. Athenaion!"

"I know that the preceding remarks are very brief. I do not need to speak in detail because a learned person like you does not need a detailed analysis or elucidation of these ideas. I made them only to highlight facts not many people seem to see, much less acknowledge, that the economic elite that rules them does not perform its governance directly by sitting in the chair of the president, the king, the judge, the legislature, the prime minister, the CEO of the big corporations, the chancellor of universities, the bishop, or the general of the army, but by manipulating these leaders the way an artist manipulates a marionette. They do this by controlling their budgets. Their budget is the throat through which they breathe the air of life, of existence. Choke this throat, and you destroy the institution."

"I have listened to your lecture on the political ideas of Machiavelli and Hobbes. They were a naïve adumbration of the assumptions that underlie them. They are based on what human beings have done, not on what they can do, and not on what they should do. Their view of human nature is limited. The human essence is an infinite possibility of realization, of growing in its powers of knowing, valuing, choosing, and creating the good and the beautiful. You seem to be stuck in the fifteenth-century mentality. The power of technology you have naively referred to a minute ago, which is the child of the creative labor of reason, is slowly unleashing these powers. Technology is a double-edged sword. It can be used for the purpose of good or bad. Why not use it for a good purpose? The good is, by its very essence, more desirable, more appealing, and more glorious than the bad, which is you. *To be is good, not to be is bad*! You are the god of nothing."

"I am bad. I shall promote the cause of badness because this is my essence, this is my destiny, and I intend to realize my destiny with all my knowledge, all my skills, and all my powers.

"And now?"

"Now, I plan to undermine your work on the human community project."

"I have a clearer picture of your design and maybe the way of implementing it."

"Good. Slowly, and in the slyest possible way, the economic elite will commit the crime of the millennium." Dr. Athenaion fired a look of inquiry at Mowt's face. She never heard this expression and desired to know its meaning and implications. "They have already embarked on the transvaluation of the values that are dear to your heart. Yes, the same values that gave impetus, nourishment, and momentum to human civilization during the past few millennia: wisdom, love, truth, beauty, peace, progress, respect for human life, freedom, and human happiness. Human beings grow and become more complete the more they expand the realization of these values in their individual lives. Now, let me rhetorically ask you, What ideals motivated and guided the scientist, the philosopher, the artist, and the social reformer over the past three thousand years? What has been the main subject of the teacher, the parent, the priest, the legislator, *but* these values and the urgent need to live according to them?"

"But, cast an investigative, honest, yes, honest, and truly rational look at people in the real streets of practical life and observe whether they know the meaning and significance of these values? If you do, you will discern that they do not give a hoot about them. Except for few, truly cultivated hearts and minds like yours, and these make up a small island in a vast ocean, they are primarily interested in the essential means of survival. Living according to your values is not easy. Do you think you can easily make them stop lying, cheating, deceiving, and harming each other, or stop them from being selfish, hypocritical, and lazy? As you have argued and explained in your lectures and in your conversations with your students, human nature does not exist as a ready-made reality but as a potentiality awaiting realization. Do you think that realizing it in this world is a realistic objective? We should always remember that the human impulse is centered on biological impulse and that the biological impulse is stronger than and frequently over-rides the human impulse.

"Now, what if your plan for the development of a human community governed by technocrats is really viable, and I admit that it is in principle viable, what if it is, by a stroke of good luck or a miracle, implemented, what kind of society will it be? The Kingdom of Humanity will prevail, and that of evil will cease to exist. People like you, Dr. Athenaion, are angels of the good, the supreme good that emanates directly from the God of Love. I loathe this god, and I despise him with all my being. But I cannot allow you to continue your work on your project of a human community governed by technocrats and especially the conditions under which such a community can be established. Such a project is seductive, no less seductive than the work done by the trinity Socrates, Plato, and Aristotle and later by the Renaissance humanists. Its acceptance will signal the inauguration of the third Renaissance. I worked hard to counteract the monumental achievements of Socrates, Plato, and Aristotle and harder still to reverse the course of the European Renaissance, which reached a climax in the nineteenth century."

"How do you plan to undermine the forthcoming Renaissance?" Dr. Athenaion asked with a smirk tugging at the corner of her mouth.

"The first triumph of humanity was undermined by the fall of Athens, the second was devastated by the rise of science, and the third, which you and a few others are trying to inaugurate, will be undermined by the rise of technology. But I have been slowly and patiently creating the material conditions for the abortion of the third Renaissance before it sees the light of day for several decades now. The gradual rise of technology has enabled me to splinter the fabric of the culture of reason and human values, which I hate with every fiber of my being and which are dear to the champions of the first and second Renaissance. The fragmentation of this culture, and consequently of its spirit, necessarily entails the fragmentation of its power. For example, notice how philosophy is now divided into a multitude of schools, views, factions, and ideologies. If you ask for a definition of philosophy, of its aims, methods, or its role in human culture, you will not receive one but many definitions. Does it still have a real identity—except a kind of intellectual activity such as logical analysis, language analysis, or the superficial discussion of social and moral issues that seem to be important to the religious people and some social reformers? What about the grandiose aims proposed by the true philosophers of ancient Greece, those that have endured through the nineteenth and early part of the twentieth century? Has it occurred to you, Dr. Athenaion, that the prevailing modes of so-called philosophical activity divert the attention of the philosopher away from the moral and material progress of human beings? Can you show me a real philosopher who tries to struggle with the perennial questions of humanity?"

"But not only philosophy is divided into multiple schools, views, and trends, science and art are gradually facing the same destiny. Cast a critical, methodological look at the amazing, and sometimes baffling, proliferation of science into different types of sciences and methodologies and the differentiation of these into various sciences and methodologies. Given this proliferation, how can you produce a definition, much less a conception of science? How can science play an effective role in the advancement of human progress or the development of a human community governed by technocrats? Some of the scientists and philosophers of the past century attempted to write an encyclopedia of the unity of science and philosophy, but the project died before it was completed. Why? Philosophy paved the way for the rise of science, and science paved the way for the rise of technology, but now technology seems to lead the scientists into new ways of thinking. I doubt that it will stand on its own feet and act as a vital and constructive force in the realization of the beliefs and values you esteem so highly."

"But this fragmentation, which may not seem healthy to you, is a cancer that aims at the obstruction of any project of Love. I am slowly spreading it into every center of research, academic conferences, symposiums, and every business, as well as political and economic gatherings of scholars. I try to infuse the spirit of dissension, separation, and destruction into every union in the human world, and I seek to deconstruct everything human beings construct. For example, family has ceased to be a union founded in the bond of love. It is now a kind of partnership founded in monetary, sexual, social, and psychological interests. The church has ceased to be a union of the faithful in the body and spirit of Christ, although it appears as such a union. It is now a kind of corporation that offers certain psychological, social, political, and economic needs and services. Human freedom has ceased to denote self-fulfillment in the medium of human community. It is now freedom from the obligation to love our neighbor and to treat the promotion of human wellbeing as the central concern of our lives. Happiness has ceased to signify the joy we experience in the activity of doing something good in our lives and the lives of others. It is now the pleasure we experience when we pursue our selfish ends. Beauty has ceased to embody the experience of the aesthetic quality that enlightens the human mind and lifts it to higher modes of human living. It is now the experience of an object or event that produces pleasure. Truth has ceased to be a revelation of the essence of nature and human nature and does not encompass an adequate understanding of the social, aesthetic, political, intellectual, and moral dimensions of human life anymore. It is now the kind of opinion that justifies our personal beliefs and way of life. Peace has ceased to indicate a state of harmony. It is now the absence of conflict, violence, or any factor that disturbs the status quo. Friendship has ceased to be a human bond between two persons, one grounded in mutual respect, trust, and affection. It is now a bond founded in mutual advantage. Justice has ceased to represent a transformative power, one that meets the needs of all the citizens fairly. It is now an instrument that embodies the interests of the rich and powerful, enabling them to amass even more riches and power."

"The crime of the millennium I mentioned earlier, namely, the transvaluation of values championed by the leaders of the ancient and modern Renaissance is not yet complete. The purpose of the shortlist of transvaluations I have just mentioned, of course painfully briefly, was only to remind you because I am sure you know them quite well, for otherwise, you would not have embarked on the human community project, was intended to give an idea of the work I have been doing during the past two centuries soon after the death of that inscrutable Hegel you admire so much. This philosopher did not die early accidentally, or even naturally, but not against the laws of nature. He was a stubborn mule. Schopenhauer hated him the way I do, but he could not stop his torrential impact. I, not the spirit, will always be the moving force of the history of human civilization. The truth, which he hid from his students when he was delivering his famous lectures on the philosophy of history, and which he clothed with the concept of God, the Christian God, is that the essence of this spirit is love. This was a sneaky way to attract the approval of the philosophers and theologians of his day. But I can glean the shadow of Love, regardless of how or where he appears in this wide cosmos. I hate his god."

"Incidentally, this on-going process of the transvaluation of values is now taking place in the name of freedom, human rights, justice, love, prosperity, and respect for human individuality. These values, which are dear to your heart, will soon be replaced by the values of the almighty elite. The society that nourished your mind and heart will soon be replaced by a diversified army of technocrats representing the different types of beliefs and values of the elite. This, not wisdom, will be the architects of the future human society. You see, technology, which was viewed by idealists like you as the means by which a human community will be designed and established, is now used as a means of transforming society into a herd. They say that beauty sells, religion sells, sex sells, and now we can add one more selling commodity to this list: *humanity*. The new generation you are trying to educate is already a society of sheep. They will love you and follow you when you wear the robe of idealism because youth is innocent and naïve, but when they enter the arena of the marketplace, they will hate you and treat you as a deceiver! Don't the people around you dress, eat, think, feel, desire, hope, and seek their happiness, of course, with negligible differences, in the same way? Isn't their way of life conditioned by the economic forces of the market? Don't you think, Dr. Athenaion, that contemporary society is increasingly becoming a consuming society and that, consequently, people are gradually becoming commodities, cogs in the different types of consuming machines? Can you underestimate the influence of the media in spreading the beliefs and values of the ruling class? The teacher, the priest, the philosopher, the social reformer, and the sage used to be the source of the wisdom required to cultivate the youth and construct social and political policy. Where is this class of people? Your priest is replaced by the doctor, your teacher is replaced by the T.V. and movies, your philosopher is replaced by the academic expert, and your sage is replaced by the different technocratic committees that steer the various institutions of your society."

"The trick, which most people around you cannot see, is this: those who speak, dress, think, desire, make decisions, and plan their life-projects behave *as if* they are free human beings, but in fact, they are not free. How can they be free agents if the material and cultural conditions, the social, economic, religious, and political conditions under which they are born and in which they thrive are designed and controlled by the invisible hands of the elite? They are made to feel free without actually being free and without knowing the meaning of freedom. Has it occurred to you that the army of economists, politicians, cultural experts, educational leaders, and social scientists who analyze the concept of freedom in their articles and books and lectures do not base their analyses on the sound ontology of human nature and a worldview that reflects the inner dynamics of the powers and aspirations of humanity?"

"Money, power, sex, pleasure, and social glory, not wisdom, joy, beauty, community, and certainly not love, are the distinctive features of the society I envision. You can control those who seek survival and pleasure but not those who seek truth and love. Oh, how I loathe your God of Love!"

"Have you thought of the possibility," Dr. Athenaion, intervened, "that you would not be in my apartment this evening if your narrative is true? Could you or the universe have existed if it were not for the constructive and triumphant power of love? What is love but his creative, constructive power? What is its urge, its thrust, its supreme aim, but to forge its way into the highest possible modes of being, the kind of being that transcends the pettiness of your way of thinking and your machinations, games, and trickery? I do not know who you are, and I do not care to know whether you are a god or a phantom, stupid or intelligent, real or unreal, material or immaterial, or whether you are a foe or a friend. I do not care to know how you violated my privacy and the boundaries of my apartment. I have heard enough of your nonsense—leave!"

"But I cannot leave until— "

"Until what?"

"Until you promise to abandon your work on the human community project."

"I refuse to make such a promise."

"Don't be foolish, Dr. Athenaion!"

"If acting according to your wish is wise, I prefer to be foolish."

"Don't forget that I am Mowt, the God of Death."

"You are a travesty on human reason and human conscience."

"Aren't you afraid of death, Dr. Athenaion?"

"Not again! I will rather die than live by your rules if living by your rules is life!"

"You do not know what you are saying. Sooner or later, you will abandon your project on the development of a human community governed by technocrats. It is better to abandon it now rather than later because if you do not abandon it now, you will lose all the privileges of glory every human being around you desires."

"Do you plan to kill me?"

"I cannot do that, although I wish to kill anyone who advocates for love. I am not authorized to kill human beings—"

"And my mind?"

"I cannot kill your mind either."

"Then what?"

"I have my ways. I can create enough devastation, enough misery, enough living death, the kind that makes the greatest gods kneel before me. I can make you sizzle in the fire of death without dying, and I can make you wish you were dead many times over! I am the slyest, foxiest, most cunning god in my pantheon."

"You can practice your slyness, foxiness, and cunning if you choose to, but I shall not comply with your request."

"You will be sorry, Dr. Athenaion!"

"I prefer to be sorry rather than receive instructions or requests from a creature like you."

"We shall meet again—soon!" Mowt said and vanished.

Although Dr. Athenaion did not believe in ghosts, goblins, gods, spirits or any kind of supernatural beings, and although she was self-composed during her so-called visit with Mowt, she could not resist a surge of doubt mixed with bafflement slowly permeating her mind: "How could this being who calls himself Mowt appear and disappear and change his identity at will any time he chooses? How could he penetrate the walls of my apartment and listen to what I think and say privately and publicly? Even worse, how could he see and feel what I am thinking and feeling?" She stood before this stream of questions, not only feeling disbelief but also fear. "But is this occurrence real?" The idea that she imagined Mowt's visits crept into her mind and remaining there for a while only because these visits were contrary to reason and her sense of reality. She spent most of the evening reflecting on this most unusual experience. She found herself stuck rather tightly between the sharp claws of two hostile forces. The first was pressing her to accept the reality of this extraordinary being, which she could not do, and the second was pressing her to disbelieve its reality, which she could not do either. She was torn between the voice of reason, which was comprehensible, and the voice of the paranormal, which was incomprehensible. Nevertheless, although stuck between these two hostile environs, which was an unbearable position to be in, Dr. Athenaion decided to remain between them simply because she did not have a more desirable option.

No-one, be they family members, psychologists, colleagues, friends, or ordinary people, would take the story of Dr. Athenaion's interaction with the God of Death seriously. People enjoy watching or reading stories about supernatural people, places, and events. However, they do this for entertainment and because these stories and movies are a source of inspiration and some kind of intellectual challenge or moral enlightenment, but they would be offended if one were to report that they had had an encounter with a being such as the God of Death. Dr. Athenaion was inclined to accept the pain those jaws were inflicting on her because she felt that the truth of this bizarre and rather absurd situation will, sooner or later, be revealed. It was prudent to persevere this abnormality to the end.

But assuming this kind of attitude did not imply peace of mind, nor did it dispel the pangs of doubt from torturing her mind, because Dr. Athenaion caught herself brooding over the dramatic events of her day with an unusual emotional intensity. She tried to sleep without success. She found herself turning from one side of the bed to the other and moving from one stream of thought to another without respite. The image of her sick father and tormented mother followed by the image of Mowt pressing her to abandon her human community project, followed by the necessity to prepare her lectures for the following day and the need to perform all her obligations adequately, not to mention her anxiety over the problematic and perhaps dubious existence of Mowt—yes, these and other questions kept her awake for a long time. Although reluctantly, shortly before dawn, she went to the medicine cabinet and took a potent sleeping drug. She had no choice.

The following day, soon after she had finished her work at the college, Dr. Athenaion sped to her parent's house. Every member of the family, including Norman and Maggie, with the exception of Stanley and his father, were waiting for her. She tried to help Felicity and Maggie in the kitchen, but they declined her help. "You are more needed in the living room than in the kitchen, dear!" Felicity said. And she was right.

Three downcast faces were waiting for her when Dr. Athenaion sat next to her mother. The mere sight of that depressing spectacle produced a contrary mood in her soul. "Why all this glumness? Smile!" She said. "The world has not come to an end. We do not have a prognosis yet, and even if the news happens to be dire, this is not the way to act. Certainly, this is not the way my father would like you to react to his condition—" This exhortation was interrupted by the sound of the door opening and then closing. Dora left her seat and practically ran to the hallway. With a smile on his face, the same smile with which he greeted her every day, Henry embraced his wife in the warm circle of his arms."

"And me?" Stanley protested with a smile similar to his father's.

"And yes, you too, my dearest Stanley and all my children."

"What is the verdict?" Kenny asked after Felicity and Maggie left the kitchen and joined the family in the living room.

"So far, the cancer is restricted to the two kidneys. It has spread profusely in the right kidney, which should be excised as soon as possible, but scantily in the left. Dr. Stone and his assistant, Dr. Anton, recommended radiation treatment for the left kidney as a first step."

"How effective will it be?" Felicity asked.

"It is hard to say," Stanley said. "The probability of success is less than 50%. I am sorry to say that we do not have many options. We shall do our best!"

"But—" Felicity tried to intervene.

"There is no room for buts, dear Felicity. Diseases are produced by a complex set of chemical processes in the body. Broadly speaking, their causes, strength, and side effects differ from one body to another. One's genes and way of life play an important role in the way the body reacts to cancer. We can control some diseases, because we know their causes and how to treat them, but cancer remains a challenge."

"What do you think, Father?" Kenny asked.

"Can I or anyone else deliberate about this kind of medical circumstance? Stanley described it concisely and accurately. Our choices are nil. Dr. Stone's recommendation is realistic, but I doubt that it will produce the desired results. It originated from a scientific mind and a compassionate heart."

"When will the treatments begin, Stanley?" Dr. Athenaion asked.

"Within a few days. It seems to me that Father should take a leave of absence for the remainder of the academic year. I think the radiation treatments will be strong, and their side effects will interfere with his teaching and administrative functions."

"And me? Don't you think that I should take a leave of absence? I just cannot—"

"Please, be patient, Mother," Dr. Athenaion interjected, "step-by-step. We should not make hasty decisions. Let us first see how Father reacts to the radiation treatments."

"I agree with Anat," Stanley said and then, directing his attention to Felicity, added, "May we continue this conversation after dinner? We must all be famished."

Felicity, Dora, and Maggie left for the kitchen. Stanley, Norman, and Anat raced to the dining room and arranged glasses, mats, plates, and silverware on the table. Within a few minutes, Henry opened two bottles of wine and placed one at each side of the table. He acted as if it was just another evening, as if the cancer was not devouring his kidneys, as if he was not about to enjoy the last few meals of his life, as if he was going to continue teaching, in short, as if the procession of time halted at the door of his house. Norman watched him in astonishment as he poured the wine in the glasses. Kenny noticed this and, with a soft smile, whispered in his right ear, "This is my father! He is a flare of life, of courage, of hope!" Kenny was emotional and almost burst into tears, but stifled it with "Felicity, the table is ready!" and walked toward the kitchen. Neither Norman nor his father saw him drying his eyes on his way to the kitchen.

Dinner was a celebration of life for Dora and Henry, not only their life as husband and wife, as lovers, and as parents but also as a family. For them, family, at least theirs, is an island of human life in an ocean of social existence. They enjoyed it for its own sake, not merely as a means of survival, but because it is intrinsically valuable, because it is founded in and emanates from the love that flared in their hearts as a living fire. Can we speak of family if its members do not live from this kind of fire? Do you know that this fire is delicious, attractive, seductive and that once you taste it, you desire it again and again? You can say it is addictive! Norman, who did not live in such an island when he was an adolescent, savored the deliciousness of this fire and was seduced by its sweetness. He was stung by the sparks that flew from it in all directions. Their stings were pleasant to his heart. He did not regard Felicity as a girlfriend anymore, although she was. He began to see her from the standpoint of that fire, to understand her in the light of that fire, and to see her as the woman he loved. She was the source of this love, and he was in that love! For the first time, he began to feel at home with the Athenaions. Tell me, dear reader, how can this miraculous change happen if the person who undergoes the change does not feel those sparks? We do not love the other person through arguments, smiles, sweet words, beautiful roses, or sexual pleasure, although these are highly desirable, but because we see the light that shines in the heart of the beloved, because we feel its warmth because we relish its sweetness, because we see and understand ourselves in that light. This light is the source of the bond of love.

Norman started to follow Kenny to the kitchen, but Henry discouraged him. "The kitchen must be crowded," he said, "Dinner will be ready in a minute. Why don't you sit here next to Anat?" Stanley, who was standing next to his father, sat next to Norman. "When will I hear a performance of your symphony? I am desirous to hear a piece of your own creation!"

"My own creation?"

"Of course!"

"Works of art, philosophical ideas, and scientific hypotheses," Dr. Athenaion remarked," are frequently born in the medium of dialogue, regardless of whether it is imaginary or existential, verbal or silent. In this type of medium, the human mind rises to its highest kind of conception and creation. This is based on the assumption that, by its very essence, a dialogue is an activity of inquiry, of seeking the truth of a specific problem, question, or an aspect of experience or of the world or of expressing a certain feeling or insight that has been growing in the womb of the imagination for some time. Exchanging ideas provokes the possibility of new ideas, illumines them, and frequently offers an occasion for seeing or exploring one's biases, weaknesses, or mistakes. A family visit, one illuminated by the light of love, is, to my mind, a paradigmatic instance of spiritual dialogue."

No one, not even Norman, knew that an idea for a symphonic work was slowly bursting through the walls of his imagination that evening. It was simultaneously bursting with the surge of love that was flaming in his heart. "Where is the great work of art born, one that endures as a masterpiece, except in the bosom of such a heart? How can you arrest such a surge but by an appropriate artistic form, one that can embody its essence? I tend to think that the power of this kind of surge is the birthplace of the artwork."

"I feel the time is ripe for me to compose my first symphony. I hope that you hear it soon," Norman said reflectively. The preceding interchange was interrupted by Maggie and Felicity carrying pots of food. They were followed by Dora with a big bowl of salad. They placed the pots on the table and returned to the kitchen for more.

As it has always been at the Athenaion home, Henry began the evening meal with a toast. This time the beneficiary of the toast was Norman. "I have a wish," Henry said as he raised his glass, "that we shall hear a performance of a symphonic work by our dear Norman. I have a hunch that he is pregnant with such a symphony." All the eyes gravitated toward Norman's face with an expression of surprise on their faces. Norman, who too was surprised, felt embarrassed. Unlike theirs, his eyes were focused on Henry. "I propose a toast to the Platonic Eros, not the Freudian Eros. May this god knock at the door of your imagination, Norman, soon."

Although Henry had never proposed such a bold toast before, although it was novel, and although it was precious, it did not elicit the cheerful response it would have in the past. He pretended not to notice and, like everyone else, took a seat at the table. He ate his meal quietly and somewhat pensively. The cause of his pensiveness was not the severity of the cancer that was gnawing at his kidneys nor the imminent possibility of his death, but the gloom that radiated from the faces of his family and the dreary silence that reigned supreme in the dining room. This room had always witnessed the liveliest, most cheerful conversations the human mind desired, but not that evening. The gloom that found its way into the dining room was oppressive. He could not tolerate its sight on the faces of his family, much less feel it. No loving parent could.

When he noted that his wife and children were about to finish their meals, he spoke. "Why have you allowed gloom to enter this room and especially your minds and hearts?" He paused, scrutinized the sad faces for a few seconds, and resumed his speech, "Are you afraid that I shall suffer or that I shall die soon? Suppose I suffer the most excruciating pain, suppose I roast in the fire of this pain, suppose you watch me sizzle in it, and yes, suppose you watch one of my feet slipping into the land of death, and suppose you hear the cry of extinction streaming from my lungs, and then suppose you watch me slowly closing my lids against my will—yes, my dearest children, suppose I cease to exist, I have a strong feeling that I shall pass away soon, why should you allow gloom to even approach the door of your minds? Ask Stanley the scientist, Anat the philosopher, and Norman the artist whether the perishing that awaits everything that exists is not always around the corner. You all should know this fact. Don't cover it, not when the hand of perishing has knocked at one's door. I heard this knock, and I tend to think that you have heard it too. As your sister Anat more than once lucidly explained, perishing is inherent in the essence of things, human and natural. If this is the case, and it is, then why this gloom? Besides, I am not dead yet. On the contrary, I enjoy every moment of my life, but I shall enjoy it more profoundly and more joyfully if you smile rather than frown. You should not lose such moments. They are drops of life. Suck the joy of life from their nipples."

"I am sad, Father," Dr. Athenaion intervened, "and I could not resist the intrusion of gloom into my mind and heart not because you or we shall perish but because we shall not any more be the beneficiaries of your love and because we will not be able to love you. As you taught us, more by your actions than by your words, human love is the most precious jewel in this universe. I feel, and everyone in this room shares my feeling, that if this love is the supreme good, the good than which nothing greater can exist, then we would be foolish, heartless, and thankless if we do not agonize over your departure from this world. I do not mind losing my body to the king of perishing, but I do mind losing my human heart to him or any other king. On the contrary, I shall cling firmly to the love that gave rise to my being and the being of everything good in this universe. I shall agonize over its loss, but let me add that my agony will be sweeter than honey, and sweeter than the nectar of the gods—"

"You speak as my daughter, not as the philosopher you are. The love that energizes the cosmic process and continues to be its manager is one thing, while the love we create and promote in the lives of others is something else. No matter its kind or magnitude, love is always centered in our bodies, as Stanley has cogently argued, it will perish with the perishing of the body. Its light may endure for a while, but its rays will sooner or later pass into the realm of non-being. Nevertheless, *although it will pass away, living in its light and from it is our destiny*. Living according to its truth is what makes our lives worth living. If these remarks make sense, and I hope they do, then I beg you to cast away the gloom that fills this room. It is more desirable to invite cheerfulness in its stead. Should I remind you that it is better to leave this world with a smile than with a scowl?"

"It is not easy to do what you advise, Father," Felicity, who has been repressing a volcano of sadness in her heart, said. "I understand your advice and grasp its logic, and I think it makes sense, but it is not easy to feel and act according to its truth. No matter how truthful, how radiant, how enlightening, and how inspiring they may be, ideas remain abstract. They cannot easily change how we truly feel, especially when the object of our feeling is the death of a loving father. The death of my neighbor, a stranger, or a relative is an external event. It signifies the extinction of an 'other,' but the extinction of my dear father? That is something else. You render a great help to your family and to me when you describe your feelings about the impending approach of your death—"

"Who told you that he is going to die, Felicity?" Dora intervened. "He will not die, not now. He is not ready for it. I am not ready for it, and no one in this room is ready for it. No one in their right mind can be ready for it. Moreover, your father will go through a course of radiation treatment. I am sure he will be cured." Dora suddenly stopped and exploded into a torrent of sobs. Stanley embraced her with two compassionate eyes. He must have felt, and perhaps known, his father's intuition that he was going to die soon and that the radiation was only a last, desperate measure.

With tears in his eyes, Henry continued: "Those sobs, my love, originated from my heart, not yours, and they originated from my heart because it exists and thrives there. It has been there since the day my eyes became captive to yours. The pain you feel is my pain, but if possible, I want you to rejoice that we can sob and feel the pain of our imminent separation, for we would not feel the intensity of this pain if we were not fortunate to live a life of love? We are alive, and we should not have any sobs, regrets, or laments for as long as we are alive because, in our case, living means loving. Please, my dearest, honor this blessed moment with a smile."

"No, my Henry, you will not leave—" But Henry did not allow her to complete her sentence. He left his chair and walked to the other side of the table, where she always sat at dinner time. He placed his warm arms around her shoulders, slowly lowered his head over hers, and kissed her on the head. He let that kiss linger there for a few seconds. "I shall never leave you," he whispered in her right ear, and then he returned to his chair. While Felicity, Maggie, and Anat were weeping silently, Stanley, Norman, and Kenny were watching the spirited dialogue between Henry and Dora with astonished eyes. Witnessing a conversation of love in action is amazing, mesmerizing. It makes you a convert to the doctrine of love.

"You want to know how I feel as I stand on The Edge—correct?" Felicity, who did not yet recover from the storm of emotions that had swept through her mind during and after that dramatic scene, said, "yes, Father. I trust in your wisdom, but how do we translate the truth of your advice into a mode of action, so that our action reflects the truth?"

A life spent in love is a life that does not fear death," Henry said. "I recommend three steps for transforming this truth into action: Love! Love more! Never cease to love with all your mind and heart. Never look back and never look forward. Look into the possibility of how you can love, how you can love more, and how you can love infinitely more with all your heart and mind. If death is not perishing, if life is living from the bosom of our humanity, if this humanity is the source of human life, next, if this humanity and life *are a gift*, why should we fear death? Why should we fret or weep when our time is up? You see, transition is the most essential aspect of existence. If we recognize this fact, and it is a fact, if we participate in the rite of life, if this life is blessed by the hand of love, if we delight in the joy it produces in our hearts, why should we complain or curse the gods when it is time for us to leave? The tragedy, dear Felicity, is not leaving the world, which was ordained by the governor of the universe, but not living fully when we are alive. Do you know that many people die before they begin to live, and many more die without knowing whether they live or die?"

"I know that you are interested in how we translate this truth into an attitude *or intellectual and spiritual orientatio*n on the basis of which we make decisions, act, and react to the problems of life as rationally as we can. Our world, as your sister Anat has been arguing for some years now, does not need this flood of technological inventions, of means of entertainment, of time-killing devices, of unnecessary fantasies, of make-believe humanity, in short, of pleasure. It needs pleasure, yes, but it needs more joy than pleasure, and it needs more growth in human individuality than sheep-like human beings.

"The only power that overcomes death is the flame of life, and the only source of life is love. Did it occur to you, Felicity, and you my children, that human love is magical, that it can, by its mysterious wand, transform every moment of our lives into an eternity? Yes, love is magical. But if it can make this kind of miracle happen, if we relish such moments, and hopefully if we feel intoxicated by their relish, yet remain sober, for such intoxication is the essence of sobriety, why should we grumble when it is time for us to leave? Let me reveal to you that sometimes I had an urge to remain with you forever, but I always declined to satiate this urge because it would be a clear case of *hubris* and a foolish denial of the laws of nature. We should not allow ourselves to think this way."

"You may think that I am hasty in thinking that my days are numbered. No, I am not. When you grow older and older, you develop new capacities of thinking, feeling, and willing, and you develop new eyes and ears. You can see new dimensions of reality, especially human reality, you can hear voices coming from the depth of your own being, and you can feel the rhythm of natural life, and your personal life, more clearly and more accurately than you ever did in the past. This new type of seeing and hearing is denied to youth. I cannot hide from you the fact that I have been approaching The Edge rather fast during the past few months. The spreading cancer in my kidneys was not a surprise to me. In fact, I have been preparing myself for the end with a feeling of realism, humility, and gratitude for the life I've lived over the past seven decades. I expect the end with a feeling of inner peace, not the peace of the dead, but the peace of love. I shall end these remarks with a small request: Smile, please!"

CHAPTER FIVE

The Death of Henry Athenaion

That was Henry Athenaion's last statement on love, death, and the meaning of human life. Dora viewed it as his legacy to his children, as the core of the wisdom he accumulated throughout his life, and as an expression of his love for his family. But, except for Dr. Athenaion, it is hard to say, or even conjecture, whether the children received it as a legacy. How could it be a legacy, if Henry's love for his wife and children was a way of life? Nevertheless, it deepened their love and admiration for him not only because it was a pearl of wisdom but also because it came from an honest father. Dora was elated and, to a great extent, justified that her husband made his confession, but she was profoundly sad, indeed devastated, by the consciousness that he would soon die.

Henry submitted his request for an indefinite leave of absence to Murrah High School the following day. Dora tried to do the same with the intention of standing by his side during that trying period of their life, but her children dissuaded her from taking such a step. "Although he is your husband, although you love him profoundly, and although you share your life with him," Dr. Athenaion said to her, "he is also our father. Therefore, all of us, including Norman and Maggie, should shoulder the responsibility of easing his pain during the last days of his life. *Your love for each other does not exist only in your hearts: we are the existential embodiment of this love.* It would be a great evil, and I would add a capital crime, to watch you carry this heavy load alone. It is noble to care, Mother, but it is nobler to share." Dora was overwhelmed by that powerful expression.

"Your father, my dear, is a miracle worker," Dora responded. "I do not understand the secret of his magic, but I am convinced that the flames of his love will not die, not in my life."

Henry lived six months after that memorable testimony. The radiation treatment was ineffective, as Stanley had predicted. The spreading cancer was unstoppable. Although it was mutilating his body slowly, he was able to attend one of the most important concerts of his life. Norman did his very best to compose a symphonic work titled *The Athenaion* and perform it four months after that testimony. He was a first violinist in the Jackson Symphony Orchestra, but at that event, he was its conductor and the author of the major piece he performed. He was practically trembling when he bowed before the audience and said that the title of the major symphony they would momentarily hear, *The Aethenaion*, could also be read as *Ode to Divine Love*, the love he discovered in the Athenaion family. He also expressed his gratitude to Henry Athenaion, who not only turned on the fountain of creativity in his mind but also inspired the symphony they were about to hear. He stretched his arms toward Henry, who was sitting in a wheelchair, at the left side of the front row where his family was seated and introduced the true patron of the symphony: "This seemingly handicapped man," he said, "is a miracle worker. He was able, with the touch of the magical rod of his loving heart, to unleash the beast of creativity from the inner folds of my mind. This beast fashioned the symphony, you will hear this evening, from the tender melodies of his heart, from its noble dreams, from the passion that animates those dreams."

The short, but moving, introduction ignited a powerful wave of enthusiastic applause by the audience. Norman bowed again and stretched his arms with reverent respect toward the Athenaion family. This gesture invited another powerful wave of enthusiastic applause. Norman bowed one more time and then moved to his lectern. Tears were rolling freely over Henry's cheeks during this introduction, and they kept rolling during the performance.

One week after that magnificent performance, when the Athenaion family were finishing their evening meal, Norman left his chair and stood behind Felicity's. He placed his hands on her shoulders, pressed them with trembling fingers, and said, "Felicity and I have an announcement to make." He paused for a second, not because he was trying to elicit a dramatic reaction from the family members but because he was apprehensive, and he was apprehensive not because he was afraid of what he was about to say but because he was shy. Dora and Henry looked at him with anxious expectation, so did everyone sitting at the dining table. Norman bent over Felicity and kissed her tenderly on the head. Felicity tried to suppress the storm of emotions raging in her heart, but she could not.

On the contrary, she rose to her feet and stood next to Norman with a ruddy complexion and a joyful smile on her lips. She stole a glance at her mother and then surrendered her eyes to Norman's face. Their eyes were locked in a silent, intimate, and mystical conversation, as Dr. Athenaion later characterized it. It was followed by a mutual embrace that lasted for a rather long time. During this embrace, Felicity left a stream of happy tears on the chest of her beloved. Soon after their arms were free, albeit reluctantly, Norman pulled a small cloth pouch from the right pocket of his trousers and removed a ring from it. "This ring, my dear Felicity, is not made of gold. It is made of fire, the fire of my heart, of my love for you. Gold, diamonds, and every other precious metal, indeed everything in this world perishes, but not this kind of fire," Norman said and, focusing his attention on Dora and Henry, continued, "Let me confess to you that the flames of this fire were kindled by the love I experienced in this family. Before meeting you, I thought I was in love with your daughter, and I was honest in my love for her. But after meeting you and sharing many beautiful, exciting, warm, joyful as well as sad experiences, the love that was glowing in my heart exploded into a violent volcano. I was swept by its lava, not down the mountain but upward toward higher modes of thinking, feeling, and being. The charm of this volcano was irresistible because it was, and remains, a burst of life, the kind of life we crave as human beings, the life that makes us feel in sync with the creative impulse of the universe. Do you know that this volcano animates every organ of my body and every fiber of my mind? Believe me, if I tell you that I wish to sizzle in the fire of this volcano, not alone but in union with your beautiful, noble, and intelligent daughter. When I place this ring on her finger, and this is a symbolic act, I place my heart and so my destiny in her heart. I am not good with words, but I would be honored if you bless this engagement. I make this request only because I know that this blessing will sanctify it."

Dora and Henry blessed the engagement with their tears. Felicity practically ran to her mother, then to her father, and gave them the warmest possible hug. The scene was so dramatic, Maggie and Dr. Athenaion wept. But Felicity hugged all the men and women of the family. Before letting go of Maggie, she whispered in her ear, "Now it's your turn, Maggie!" Maggie nodded.

And Maggie kept her word. She and Kenny were engaged three weeks later. It was also blessed by the loving tears of Dora and Henry. After everyone was seated in their chairs in the living room, Kenny wondered aloud, "When shall we celebrate your engagement, Stanley, and you Anat?"

"I inspected my heart last night," Stanley responded, "to see if there were any traces of blood there, but I did not detect any on or around it. Cupid has not shot his arrow yet. I promise that you will be the first to know the moment I feel the fire of that arrow."

"You are a neuroscientist," Henry remarked, "but you are also the poet of the family. Like all the ancient Greek and Roman gods, Cupid cannot shoot his arrow randomly or capriciously, he follows the laws of nature. He will shoot his arrow into your chest at the right time and place and for the right woman, but I hope you do not try to dodge it when he does decide to shoot. You cannot afford to miss it, son. Contrary to what some critics think, it is quite possible to be a lover and a scientist at the same time. I do not need to justify this statement, but it is important to remind you of Marie and Pierre Curie." This remark came from the mind of a historian.

"You are an artist of the human heart, Father!" Stanley replied.

"I doubt that I am this or any other kind of artist, but if I were, I assure you that I owe my artistic nature to your mother. She has always been my inspiration and my teacher in the art of human living."

No one in the room made a suggestion, or a recommendation, about the possibility of Dr. Athenaion's engagement in the near or distant future only because they remembered how Dimitri, her ex-fiancé, had foolishly betrayed her and how deeply he had hurt her. But this painful experience did not mute her excitement for her sister's and brother's engagements. What mattered to her and to Stanley first and foremost was that her father was able to celebrate two of his children's engagements before his death. Besides, it was difficult for Dr. Athenaion and Stanley to think about, much less start, a romantic relationship during those six months. In addition to the heavy schedule of activities she designed for the family, which necessarily obviated the possibility of such a relationship, they were not emotionally ready for it.

During the last few months preceding Henry's death, the life of the Athenaions was punctuated by many moments of severe sadness, distress, suppressed tears, and fear. Although she devoted most of her personal time to the care of her father, Dr. Athenaion sailed through this turbulent period of her life with steadfast determination and prudent leadership. No one noticed or even felt that she was steering the ship of the family during this challenging time. On the contrary, the bond between the brothers and sisters, on the one hand, and Maggie and Norman, on the other, grew in depth and warmth. Dora noticed this development, and she delighted in it. "You are a Godsend, my dear," she said one day to her older daughter. "Your father is not dying, and he is not leaving us. He lives in us, and he will stay with us. I see the glow of this truth every time I speak or reminisce with him about our lives. He feels that God does not exist in some heaven, some infinity, or some metaphysical realm, but is, instead, here on earth in our hearts. This is where he is going to stay after his body splinters into thin air."

"But my father's love does not exist only in our hearts. It will also be a torch that guides our lives. I have already witnessed the truth of this torch. Did creativity explode in Norman's imagination by accident? Was he inspired to compose *The Athenaion* by accident? Was his teaching, which inspired many a student to go to university, and many more to become doctors and lawyers, an accident? Was his contribution to the reconstruction of the curriculum at Murrah an accident? Did the love that flared in Felicity's, Norman's, and Maggie's hearts like a shining sun happen by accident? Now I see clearly that everything I do is quietly inspired by your and my father's love for each other and for us."

"Do you know," Dora confessed, "that more than once I willed my death and prepared myself for burial with your father soon after he made his last testimony? Yes, I willed to die and let me tell you that death can be willed. But, having reflected on the message of his testimony and particularly on the way you and the rest of the extended family rose willingly to be by our side when death overpowered your father's body, I came to the conclusion that it is wiser to live and feel his presence and yours rather than die. Death is not the death of our bodies, as your father has reminded us more than once, it is the death of the human heart, of the life that emanates from this heart."

"*The Athenaion* will not only be the title of Norman's first symphony, but it will also be the title of my project on the development of a human community governed by technocrats. The legacy of love you and Father have bequeathed to us, and many other people will remain a radiant presence for a long time."

"There is one thing that disturbs me about the way your father decided to leave the world."

"What is it, Mother?"

"As you recall, he did not wish anyone, except his nuclear family and now the extended family, to be present at his funeral. I wonder whether this decision was justifiable. Many of our colleagues and friends strongly desired to say farewell to a man they respected, but they could not. 'We loved him dearly,' Mr. Denny, our Principal, told me. 'We shared many good and bad times. He was a most valuable asset to Murrah. I wish I could see him before he leaves us permanently.' This same sentiment was expressed by several colleagues and neighbors."

"Did you discuss this with Father?"

"Yes, I did. In fact, he raised it a few months before he knew he was going to die soon."

"Did he give you any explanation?"

"Yes, he did."

"Is it confidential?"

"No, my dear. He said that one's death is not and cannot be a public rite because the experience of dying and death cannot be shared. It is absolutely personal. People may know in general what it means to die, and they may view it as a significant occurrence, but they cannot comprehend the meaning of a particular person's death because it is not shareable. They can understand, to a reasonable extent, the meaning of events such as birthdays, sickness, or different types of traumatic experiences, but not death. Only the person who lived life can understand the meaning of that life and, therefore, of its extinction. Even if they are allowed to peek through some magical window to witness how a dying person feels or acts, their knowledge of what they witness will remain objective, external, indirect, and so incomplete, because it is extremely difficult to communicate how the dying person feels. The subjective experience is an experience of 'me,' 'mine,' 'I'; such an experience is not communicable. I may tell you how I feel in general by using labels such as 'sad,' 'depressed,' or 'devastated' when my son, wife, or friend dies. However, I cannot communicate the depth, richness, or uniqueness, nor the experience itself, in a way that allows you to see, feel, and comprehend *what* and *how* I feel. In addition to the subjectivity of human feelings, we should always remember that the dying person is a human world of religious, political, social, intellectual, cultural, and aesthetic experiences. This world is unique; it is neither repeatable nor communicable.

How can anyone, be they philosophers, psychologists, or sociologists, open a window in the wall of one's subjectivity? We may succeed in communicating, through concepts, some aspects or dimensions of the experience, but this kind of communication is conceptual, general, not existential, or factual. Is it an accident that a multitude of artworks, especially in the area of the novel, revolve and frequently dance around it, the theme of life, death, and love, but cannot capture or communicate their essence or the *fullness of their being and meaning*? We feel gratified if a work provokes an insight or a new way of thinking or understanding of what it means to live, to die, and to love, but we cannot hope for more. Again, observe how mourners behave in funeral homes, private homes, or condolence parlors—what do they talk about or think, at such places? Most of the time they speak hypocritically on a specific part or action of the dead person's life, career, social life, wealth, or some of his adventures, about the flowers that cover the coffin, about the events of the day, about the gossip or scandals of the day *but never about death, what it means to die, or the meaning of human life*. But what is comical about these visitations is that the dead person has already ceased to exist. Accordingly, can we say that these visitations are for the living and not for the dead? Your father shunned them like the plague."

"But how did he feel about the presence of his family at his funeral?" Dr. Athenaion asked. "If I am not mistaken, he desired our presence. He also insisted that Maggie and Norman attend it."

"Yes, I asked him this question. As you would expect, the basis and justification of this desire, and he used the word 'justification' with emphasis, is the love in which we are united as a family. Among other things, he emphasized that his life was an open book to us. He did not hide anything from us. For him, the moment of leaving this world required our presence because we are united in the human bond of love, because he wished to feel the fire of this love, because he felt an obligation to drink one more cup from it, for he treated that moment as a kind of Holy Communion, and because, for some mystical reason, he felt that our presence is the reason for his being Henry Athenaion in this world. I have a feeling that he treated our presence at his funeral as a celebration of love, of life—"

"A celebration?" Dr. Athenaion asked, interrupting her mother.

"Yes, as a celebration."

"Did he explain the sense in which it was a celebration?"

"Not directly, but I could infer from what he said that it was a celebration of love, not different from the ones we used to have during our family visits."

"Amazing! Did he express any regrets?"

"Frankly, my dear, I asked him this very question—"

"What was his response?"

"'I was granted the privilege to celebrate the rite of life for almost seven decades. I know I was not asked whether I wished to be invited to this *cosmic banquet* or to be born. I also know that the opportunity to love and be loved is the greatest gift any human being can dream of. Finally, I know that perishing is an essential, perhaps the most essential aspect of existence. Therefore, my sojourn on this earth would be short. Yes, if I possess this knowledge, Dora, why should I regret leaving this world? Do I have a right to complain? No. I have a right to feel sad, infinitely sad, and I do, only because I desire to remain with you, but I do not have a right to complain.' This was your father's answer to my question. I agree with him. Why should he have any regrets if I, your mother, was his love, his heart, and his life? Why should he have any regrets if he had these wonderful children? Why should he have any regrets if he was able to serve society to the best of his ability? I tend to think, Anat, that the ancients did not create gods of love in response to a sudden whim or some capricious desire but as a response to a deep craving in human nature, and I am not too much amiss if I add that this craving is the most profound impulse in human nature. I feel, and this is only a feeling, that, no matter their intellectual, artistic, scientific, philosophical, or practical achievements, no matter the significance of the role these accidents play in the life of human civilization, people will feel a painful measure of loneliness if they do not satiate this craving."

"Father discussed this last point in his last conversation, but his discussion was brief. I wonder whether he discussed with you in some detail why those who live from the fountain of love do not feel regrets when they leave this world."

"Yes, we discussed it on more than one occasion. I cannot repeat what he said verbatim, but I can communicate his view in my own words and according to my own understanding of it."

"Excellent! I simply wish to know his view, Mother," Dr. Athenaion requested.

"People who live in bad faith, that is, who do not grow in and live from the essence of their humanity, who do not live according to the values that are founded in the basic needs of our humanity, in short, who sell their soul to the world, tend to feel guilty when they reach the end of the line."

"Why, Mother?"

"When you neglect the basic human needs, you neglect yourself, and if you neglect yourself, you live in bad faith. Living in bad faith is the source of regret or guilt."

"How?"

"'Bad faith' is the opposite of 'good faith.' People live in good faith inasmuch as they meet the essential needs of human nature, the biological, intellectual, emotional, aesthetic, and spiritual needs. Except for the biological needs, the realization of human needs is always a possibility for further realization, mainly because their bases exist in human nature as potentialities of infinite realization. Therefore, human destiny consists of human growth and development, not necessarily in reaching a certain point of perfection. Those who lead a life of growth tend to feel peace when they are about to depart his word."

"The point warranting special attention here is that people are human individuals inasmuch as their deeds or accomplishments are abundant and inasmuch as they succeed in realizing the greatest measure of their potentialities. Prior to its realization, a potentiality is merely a schema, an idea, or a plan of action. As such, it is existentially empty. It becomes real when it is realized, that is, when the potentiality is transformed into an action or a mode of behavior. The individual feels fulfilled while in the process of realizing their potentialities because every realization, or action, signals an addition to the pre-existing self. Consequently, the more that human potentialities are realized, the more the human self grows. What is fascinating, indeed mysterious, is that people realize their human potentialities more proficiently as they grow. Don't we grow in wisdom when we grow in knowledge and experience? Don't artists grow in their ability to feel the world and express its meaning more deeply, more effectively, when they create more works of art? Accordingly, yes, my dear Anat, I do not exaggerate if I say that people who live in good faith, who are faithful to themselves as human beings, act from their minds, hearts, and wills, not from an external authority such as society, theologians, god, sages, the state, or a specific ideology. I have a feeling that this is the main reason why your father felt inner peace when he discovered that his kidneys were being devoured by cancer. Why should he have any regrets if the life he led was authentic, fulfilled?

"But, on the other hand, people who live their life in bad faith will necessarily feel regret when they reach the last station of their lives. When you neglect your true self, the self that is founded in the beliefs and values that define your true essence as a human being, you marginalize it, you put it on hold, you suppress it, you borrow, steal, or rent a self that is not you. You live according to the beliefs and values of the herd, of the invisible 'they.' Your self becomes an extension of the invisible, non-existent, 'they,' in short, you become a hollow being. Your true self remains unfulfilled. The sad thing is that when you live according to the beliefs and values of the 'they,' you convince yourself that you are doing well. You deceive yourself by thinking that everybody lives this way, everybody appears happy, and you argue that if everybody lives this way and is happy, I too should be living well and must be happy. You hear the voice of your conscience, the conscience of your true self once in a while, at the end of the day, on a weekend, or when you face a serious problem, asking you to meet your human needs, to be yourself, but you silence this voice by a small injection of pleasure—by going to a party, watching a movie, going on a vacation, or visiting a friend."

"You see, a life lived in bad faith does not originate from the mind and will of the person. The true self remains a potentiality that cries for realization and is, therefore, existentially empty. The feeling of this emptiness, which surges into our consciousness occasionally, is the source of the regret people feel when they reach the end of their lives. Such people discover, rather late, the truth of their phony life, which was no life. Confronting the emptiness that fills their being is, your father insisted more than once, the main source of the regrets and guilt people feel at the end of their lives. What makes this realization acute is that they cannot do anything about it because *the flow of time is irreversible.* How many times have you heard retired people, terminally ill people, or incapacitated people say, 'If I had my over life again, I would live it quite differently!' or 'I wish I could live my life again!', and so forth. Yes, Anat, a life lived in bad faith, is a life that dies in guilt, in regrets."

"Did Father speak of redemption?"

"Yes, my dear, he did."

"Is it possible for a person who lived in bad faith to find some measure of peace, some kind of redemption—a little, just a little? I ask this question because losing one's life is a capital crime. Can such a crime be redeemed? A little—maybe a little."

"How?"

"A wasted life cannot be redeemed because it cannot be recovered. Your father emphasized to me more than once that nothing can be recovered from the belly of the past. The past is a wasteland—a graveyard! If redemption is at all possible, the person who feels the pangs of guilt acutely should rise to their feet and spend their remaining days as productively as constructively as possible. This assumes that it is never too late to do the good in one's life and the lives of others. Doing good is not only the source of a life worth living but also of redemption. The feeling of guilt may never leave the guilty mind, but the flames of the goodness that thrives in it and will necessarily temper it and enable it to feel a reasonable measure of peace."

A different conversation was awaiting Dr. Athenaion after she left her mother. The lights were on when Dr. Athenaion arrived at her apartment. She was not surprised! "He is in," she conjectured. Indeed, he was waiting for her in the living room, sitting on the sofa in the same place and the same position. She stood behind the reclining chair that faced the sofa and whirled an angry look at him. She was about to scold him and instantly dismiss him from her apartment, but he intercepted her attempt with a sardonic greeting: "What nobility, what idealism, what magnanimity!" This remark was Mowt's response to her conversations with her parents. He stopped for a second and then continued, "Please, Dr. Athenaion, sit. I have missed our conversations. Sit! Feel at home! You are at home!" He added sarcastically.

"You are not welcome in this home, and this is not your home. Do not act as if you are its master. You are a bundle of nothing!" She said with a frown on her forehead.

"I am not as bad as you think."

"You are the worst. You cannot see, much less comprehend, the magnitude of your evil."

"Why don't you sit? Can we have a rational conversation?"

"With you?"

"Yes, have you forgotten that I can act like a human being and assume the identity of any type of philosopher or scientist or artist? It has been a great pleasure to converse with the most distinguished philosopher in Jackson, Mississippi, and it will always be a pleasure to converse with you."

"Stop this rubbish! Nothing but evil comes from the source of evil." Unaware of what she was doing, Dr. Athenaion slipped into the reclining chair.

"I am the God of Death and the nephew of the Devil," Mowt retorted. From your point of view, I am the source of the greatest evil in the universe, but from my point of view, I am the source of the greatest good. How can I be evil if I follow the laws that created the universe?"

"You do not follow the laws of the universe. The highest law of the universe emanates from the power that has created the universe, the same law that underlies the progress of human civilization. You do not seem to realize that being is good, and non-being is bad, and you do not seem to realize that the highest manifestation of being is life, and the highest manifestation of life is humanity. How can the force that aims at the destruction of human life speak of good, reason, or rational conversation? You cannot speak, you babble!"

"This is my nature. I exist for the express purpose of undermining the works of the God of Love: *humanity.* This type of reality is the sun of the universe. My aim is to eclipse it, and I shall not hesitate or procrastinate in my endeavor to achieve my purpose. Let me reaffirm to you that I hate the light; I love to exist in the dark. The spectacle of love you and your father initiated during the past several months was bright, very bright. I cannot stand it!"

"I frequently stood at the gate of Plato's Cave,—the cave your favorite philosopher described eloquently, insightfully, and powerfully—and barred any of the dwellers inside from trying to escape and ascend to the world of the Sun, the sun you endear so much, the sun you contemplate when you crave inspiration and understanding. The vast majority of the human race lives in this cave. They are happy there. Why should you burden their minds with big ideas and their hearts with noble emotions? Don't you think that a few drops of pleasure and peaceful existence is enough?"

"You should dwell in that cave and stay there forever! You are not created to see the light of the sun!"

"Yes, you can metaphorically say that I am the God of the Dark! This is exactly why I cannot allow you to irradiate the light of The Sun. Your father was the brilliant star of the family, now it is your mother. Very soon, the Athenaion family will be a tribe, which will erect a citadel of humanity. Its members will be disciples of love. They will carry the book of the God of Love in one hand and the book of human community in the other. Your vision of this community may not be realized in your lifetime, but it will be realized by your followers after you die. But you will not die because you will live in that community the way your father lives in you and your growing family. The mere thought of this possibility makes me cringe, but I do not like to cringe. I am the God of Death, not of life!"

"I am not interested in how you feel or what you aim at. I am impatient with your jabber! Let me assure you that I shall not desist from developing my project on the development of a human community governed by technocrats."

"I have underestimated you, Dr. Athenaion; you are more stubborn than I thought—"

"You do not seem to distinguish between a person who clings to a belief because it is true, who knows the meaning and significance of truth, who respects it, and acts according to it freely and a person who clings to a belief blindly, foolishly, without knowing why they cling to it or because the belief is a fixture in their mind. The first type of person knows that knowledge of the truth and acting on it is essential to *human living*, the second does not know how or why they cling to their belief or why they exist."

"I detest your way of human living!" Mowt exclaimed.

"How can you detest my way of life if you are a drop of detestation? Your presence, your speech, your smell are wafts of loathing."

"Do you know that the more I converse with you, the stronger my desire becomes to obstruct your project on a human community governed by technocrats?"

"Enough! Leave this apartment!"

"I cannot leave until you promise to abandon your project."

"Leave immediately!"

"I admire your self-confidence. But confidence is not enough. Let me ask you this. 'Are you willing to give up all the pleasure, knowledge, beauty, glory, power, sex, wealth, and fame in this world for the sake of reason and love?'"

"You and all your bounties are empty vanities. You should know, if you can know, that reason and love are not for sale, and if they are not for sale, I am not for sale!"

"You astonish me, Dr. Athenaion, but people are for sale, and they are commodities in the market of social existence. Even the gods of the ancient Egyptians, Greeks, Romans, and Persians were commodities. All creatures are commodities and are, therefore, for sale. You are a creature; therefore, you are for sale," Mowt paused, threw a sarcastic look at Dr. Athenaion, and continued: "Reason and love are for sale. Nothing in the universe exists as an end in itself, as you are in the habit of saying, that is, as absolutely valuable. I am the prime salesman of people, love, and true ideas, and I am the snoop of the human race. I constantly pry into the minds, hearts, and souls of your humanity. Let me assure you that, except for a few people, such as the cursed Socrates, all the human beings who left their mark on the history of civilization were, in principle, for sale. I could have bought any one of them for a price. Life is dearer than anything in the scheme of nature, and human life is dearer than anything in the human world. Anyone of those great, noble, and magnanimous human beings you seem to admire so much, would tremble and fall apart the moment I seduce them or allow them a vision of their death. What makes you think you are an exception?"

"Those few people you referred to, and they are not few, will remain the lighthouse of reason and love. One sun is enough to illuminate the world! This sun can be the source of the human life you seem to detest!"

"Are you sure?"

"From the fact that some human beings are commodified, it does not necessarily follow that human beings are commodities, and from the fact that reason and love are or can be commodified, it does not necessarily follow that they are commodities. Even if a human being is used as a slave by a tyrant, that slave is a human being. Neither you nor any of your gods can change that fact. The human essence can never be a commodity because it contains its infinite value within itself. Humanity does not derive its existence and value from you or creatures like you but from the God of Love!"

"You have lost your patience with me, but I have not lost my patience with you. It has been my policy to rely on the method of persuasion to achieve my aims. I promise I shall adhere to this policy to the end. I assure you that sooner or later you shall abandon your glorious project! Contrary to what you think, you are a stubborn philosopher!

"A stubborn being who sees herself as stubborn ceases to be stubborn."

"Why?"

"Because stubbornness is ugly, repulsive. Look at yourself in the mirror. If you do, you will know what I mean," Dr. Athenaion said sarcastically. "You are more pitiable than admirable."

"You are beginning to get on my nerves! Don't let me lose my patience!" Mowt hesitated, then added threateningly, "I shall be back. This time I hope to receive a positive answer from you!"

"Never!"

Mowt vanished without saying a word.

CHAPTER SIX

The Eminent Dr. Athenaion in Jail

The tree of love Henry Athenaion planted in the hearts of his children during his lifetime grew and flourished after his death. Norman introduced his parents, David and Charlotte Mackenzie, to Dora and her children. David was a gemologist. In addition to a degree in geology he received from Union College, he attended the Institute of Gemology in Chicago. His first son, Danny, succumbed to incurable poliomyelitis shortly after he was born. Charlotte, who received a theology degree from Belhaven College and was planning to become a minister in the Presbyterian Church, abandoned her plan and decided to devote her life and energy to the care and cultivation of her son, Norman. She did not want to lose him. She stood by his side until he graduated from Belhaven College and joined the Jackson Symphony Orchestra as a first violinist. She and David were elated when they learned that Norman would lead the Orchestra with a symphony he composed. Being a composer was Charlotte's innermost but silent desire. She felt justified in abandoning the ministry and preparing her son for a creative life in music. She and her husband felt that, although they have not yet met them, they were closer to the Athenaions than to their own relatives. The transformation of their son's purpose from being a violinist to being a composer, from being an ordinary person to being an artist after he met Felicity, was astonishing, admirable, indeed miraculous! Charlotte was ecstatic to know that her son was engaged to a young woman like Felicity!

Maggie introduced her mother, Antoinette Sargento, and her sister Brenda to Dora and her children. Antoinette lost her husband to a ferocious cancer tumor in the brain when his daughters were teenagers. She was never re-married. She was a ceramist and was recognized as one of we most respected ceramists in the city of Jackson. Brenda was the manager of the women's clothing section at Macrae's Department Store. She had received a degree in English from Union College and was hoping to seek a graduate degree in English literature, but was unable to realize her purpose for financial reasons, and had accepted a temporary position in the Jewelry department at Macrae's. The store manager was so impressed with her communication and organizational skills that he had asked her to be the manager of the women's clothing section of the store. He doubled her salary with a hefty annual bonus, which no graduate in management could refuse, and Brenda did not refuse it. Maggie joined her mother at the pottery immediately following her graduation from Mississippi College with a degree in sociology. In fact, Kenny met Maggie at the showroom of the pottery. He was looking for a present for a colleague who was getting married the following Sunday. She had just returned from the potter's wheel when he had entered the showroom. He smiled when she welcomed him and wondered whether she could help him. Instead of responding to her verbally, he smiled, and his smile was tender and compassionate, as she had remarked later. He did not respond to her question immediately because his eyes forbade his lips from speaking; they were beguiled by her face. She did not know how to react to his gaze, but she was not offended by it either because it did not signify malice. How can you be offended by a tender and compassionate gaze?

Nevertheless, her reaction did not prevent her from being confused. Fortunately, her confusion did not last long, for he suddenly thrust his hand into the right pocket of his jacket in search of a napkin, but the pocket was empty. He bit his lower lip softly, and then without hesitation, he stretched his right hand toward her forehead. She reflexively thrust her head backward. The smile returned to his lips as his hand was again aiming at her forehead and said as he was wiping away shining clay particles which dotted her forehead and which must have flown from the potter's wheel a few moments ago, "Please don't be afraid. I just cannot allow these clay particles to smear your beautiful face!" Involuntarily, Maggie stroked her forehead and gaped into his smiling face. His smile invited a shy yet graceful smile to her lips. Those two smiles must have met in the space that separated them and united them in the fire of an intimate moment, one that lasted forever.

Kenny and Maggie announced their wedding six months after the death of Henry Athenaion. The announcement was delayed until then, only because the Athenaion family was in mourning. But the waiting period was hard for the lovers. They felt an ardent desire to be united in body and soul as soon as possible. They simply could not understand why they should live under separate roofs if love was growing in their hearts faster than the speed of light. "Should mourning for my father stop me from loving you?" Kenny intimated to Maggie one afternoon when they were rambling in the Petrified Forest near Yazoo City. "He is in my heart, and I shall always mourn his death. Shouldn't morning be a celebration of love?"

"Tradition!" Maggie remarked.

"Tradition is a mode of behavior or practice imposed by the social or religious establishment, or by culture. But genuine mourning is a personal matter. Besides, it is a subjective feeling. It is private and confidential. No one can either control or supervise this kind of feeling. Tradition should not regulate how or how long an individual should mourn their loved ones. This feeling cannot be dictated by an external authority, regardless of whether it is social, religious, or cultural. What if I did not love my father, can tradition make me love him? How can it reward me or punish me if I mourn or refrain from mourning for him? I tend to think that genuine mourning originates from the depth of the human heart. It differs from—"

"But we can love each other even when we are grieving for your father. Grieving and loving are not mutually exclusive of each other. Indeed, genuine grieving should intensify our love for each other, my dearest, don't you think?" Kenny agreed with a thoughtful look emanating from his eyes. "Your father used to characterize love as a flame of fire. I now think that this characterization was not metaphorical but literal, because the flame of our love is raging wildly in my heart. I think this flame is confounding my sense of time. If only you know how strongly I wish I can jump over the stream of time and stand next to you and, with you, in the chapel of Union College now instead of a few weeks from now! Do you know that during the day, I feel as if I am walking on fire, and during the night, I feel like I am sleeping in a bed of fire? The sting of this fire is sweet to my heart, and it will be sweeter, much sweeter when you walk with me in the day of our lives and sleep with me in the night of our lives? This fire is my home. I wish that I can live in this home forever!" Kenny moved closer to his beloved and embraced her, then he returned her yearning look with one of his own, and said:

"The fire that flames in your heart are the fire of my heart, the same fire you kindled in it. I too sizzle in it and wish to live in it forever." Maggie freed herself from his arms and embraced him. Tears of joy were rolling over her ruddy cheeks. They landed on his neck.

"I would be gratified if the fire of our love confused my sense of time—"

"Why?" Kenny wondered teasingly. "I ask, even though I feel your feeling."

"Because then we shall be able to live within the frame of our time. We cannot influence the flow of natural time, but we can create and structure our own frame of time according to the desire of our hearts! We shall be able to transform every moment of ordinary time into eternity. Do you know, Kenny, that it feels as if I already feel the pulse of this eternity in my heart and mind?" She paused for a second and added, "Yes, I do!" But the lovers had to defer the announcement of their wedding to the first Sunday that followed the mourning period.

Dora's house was changed into a salon every Sunday afternoon. The Athenaion mini clan met as a family during that time. They cooked and enjoyed a good supper and then reviewed the political and social news of the week, talked about their personal problems and adventures, as usual, and discussed some of the critical intellectual questions in religion, science, psychology, and philosophy. This period gradually became a kind of cultural and social haven. Dora did her best to foster an atmosphere tolerance, compassion, trust, and mutual respect in her extended family. Maggie, who understood and appreciated the moving spirit of the Athenaions, remarked in a conversation with Brenda, shortly after the mourning period was over, that Dora was not only Henry's wife but also an emanation of his spiritual presence, one that continued to radiate love. "He really believed," she emphasized, "that most human problems could be solved in the spirit of love. If only people grasped the full meaning of this gem of wisdom! I sometimes feel, when I am in a pessimistic mood, that the wheels of cosmic love—of justice, cooperation, compassion, creation, and mutual respect—have been grinding slowly, ever so slowly, throughout human civilization. I am fortunate to have met Kenny and his family. Do you know that I have met him through his family and his family through him?"

But this intimate conversation between the two sisters was interrupted by Kenny's sudden appearance. He stood behind his fiancé and placed his hands over her shoulders. Maggie thought that he was about to announce the date of the wedding, but she was mistaken. "Anat has not arrived yet," he said and then squeezed her shoulders softly. She understood the significance of that squeeze. She slid out of the corner of the sofa and stealthily walked with Kenny to Felicity's bedroom. "It seems that the philosophy department at Union will be closed. Anat will be out of a job at the end of next month."

"Do you mean that the entire philosophy program will be removed from the curriculum?"

"They kept a few service courses such as Logic, Ethics, and Problems of Philosophy, but not enough to constitute a major. I am worried about my sister. She has been trying for several months to save the philosophy program but to no avail. The college has been practically bankrupt for more than six years. Instead of improving, the financial condition of the college has been getting exceedingly worse. What is distressing is that Anat contacted several colleges and asked if she could apply for a position. She discovered that they were facing similar financial difficulties—"

"Why?" Maggie asked, interrupting Kenny.

"I cannot give you a detailed account. Anat briefly mentioned two reasons. The first is "marketability." Many colleges, even liberal arts colleges, are required to justify their existence, that is, their continuation or elimination, on the criterion of marketability. The existence of a program is justifiable inasmuch as it is marketable. The aim of higher education is not the cultivation of human character, the expansion of the horizons of knowledge, the exploration of the conditions of the moral or spiritual progress of society, or the preparation of the students for enlightened citizenship anymore, but the advancement of the economic, military, and political health of the state."

"And the second reason?"

"Administrative and teaching incompetence and depravity and ideological clannishness."

"Ideological clannishness—do you mean the way it used to be practiced in the Soviet Union and the rest of the ideologically governed states?"

"Yes, but in a different way. We need to discuss this question in detail in the next few weeks."

"Why not change the incompetent faculty and administrators?"

"That is a good question. It is not easy to remove tenured faculty or weak administrators. The new president thought that the best way to get rid of the tenured faculty is to close the department. I really think, my dear, that we should discuss this problem in some detail in the next few weeks.

"Yes," Maggie said, a pensive expression on her face. We should remain by Anat's side during this trying period in her life." Maggie felt that

Kenny was seriously worried about his sister. On the other hand, she too was seriously worried about Anat, not because she was merely the fiancé of her brother or her prospective sister-in-law but primarily because she felt she was her sister

"We should!" Kenny murmured.

"Maybe I am needed in the kitchen," Maggie responded, embracing him warmly.

But the kitchen was crowded, and the crowd was enjoying themselves. They were preparing the evening meal studiously but were also having a social visit. Brenda was mincing cucumbers, tomatoes, parsley, mint, and green peppers for Armenian salad. Everyone was listening attentively to her description of how she met Dimitri Flack, Anat's ex-fiancé, at Macrae's bridal shop. He was helping his sister, Sally, select her wedding gown. She must be getting married. "He used to be the most handsome man in Jackson," Charlotte remarked, "I wonder whether his beauty faded and whether he is still single."

"Oh, no," Brenda said, "he is still an image of masculine beauty. You should have been in the store to see how some of the saleswomen were parading the shop and sneaking admiring looks at him."

"Do you know if he is still single?"

"He must be because he was alone with his sister," Brenda remarked.

"Physical beauty is not everything," Antoinette intervened, "real beauty is inner beauty—of the mind, of the heart, of the entire person. Spiritual beauty beautifies the body! The beauty of the body without the beauty of the soul is, to my mind, a curse, hell on earth! A woman like Anat cannot be interested in Dimitri's kind of beauty, regardless of how impressive or desirable it might seem!"

"I agree with you, but unfortunately, nowadays, we live in a world of physical beauty, the kind that pleases your eyes, not your mind, not your soul. Mere physical beauty is surface beauty, not human beauty. The human heart cries for human beauty!"

"Let me tell you," Antoinette said, expanding the same idea, "intelligent women would sooner or later discover the nature and true value of real beauty. These women aim at life, not at appearance, and certainly not at deception. Was it an accident that Anat dismissed Dimitri from her life the moment she discovered that he was cheating on her? Living with a fraud is worse than living with the devil."

"But—" Charlotte started to speak but did not complete her statement.

"But what?" Felicity asked, curious to know what was on Charlotte's mind.

"What if Dimitri has changed? What if he asks for an audience with Anat, genuinely repents, and asks for another chance? Should she take him seriously?"

"Is it a question of asking for another chance," Felicity wondered, "or a question of healing a deeply wounded soul? How can you heal such a soul? How can you heal a soul that was betrayed, a soul that is now bereft of itself?" Felicity paused for a moment and added, "How can you put a soul in a soul-less body? Can you? If you can, how do you achieve such a task? How can you extricate the cancerous worm of vanity from a weak, depraved person?"

"Let me express a wild opinion, Felicity—"

"I like wild opinions!"

"A wounded soul is torn between two antithetical yet unwavering feelings—an unwavering feeling for the beloved she has lost and an unwavering repulsion for him. She does not want to lose the man she had thought was a genuine human being, and she cannot bear the feeling that he proved to be a fraud. Therefore, I raise the question of the possibility of reconciliation. Some men, and women too, are willing to repent and change the way they think, feel, and what they want from love and life. Let me tell you that reformed men are sometimes the most loving husbands you can imagine."

Felicity could not respond to Charlotte's wild opinion, for a commotion in the living room was already coursing through the kitchen. "Anat is here. We can now begin," Dora said with an eager voice. She moved the squash casserole she had prepared, to the dining room. Felicity, Maggie, Charlotte, and Antoinette moved the rest of the pots.

Two announcements were supposed to be made when the Athenaion family finished their supper that evening, the first by Kenny and the second by Dr. Athenaion. Kenny, who knew about his sister's imminent termination from her position as a full-time faculty member at Union College, decided to go first. "Maggie and I have agreed to be married in this house a few weeks hence. The wedding will be a family event. It will be a joyful moment, but the prospect of sharing it with you, who is dearer to our hearts more than anything in this world, will transform this joy into the most precious gift we can hope for!" Maggie rose to her feet and walked to Dora, hugged her tightly, and said, "You are the greatest blessing in our lives, Mama," and with tears in her eyes, she added, "I am fortunate to have two mothers." She walked to her mother and gave her an equally tight hug. That hug was consecrated by a flood of tears. Gladness filled the dining room.

Alas! Dr. Athenaion, who was planning to announce the closing of her department and her termination from the college as a faculty member, decided to remain silent. She simply could not contaminate the air of mirth everyone was enjoying. On the contrary, she cherished that feeling. Nevertheless, Stanley, who besides Kenny, understood why she did not make the announcement, came to her rescue just before the family was about to leave the dining room for a general visit and conversation in the living room. He left his chair and stood behind his sister's. "Anat," he said, "will be leaving her position as a professor of philosophy at Union College at the end of this semester. The college has decided to shut down the philosophy department. Other departments will also be shut down. Union has been bankrupted for several years now." The air of mirth that filled the dining room a little earlier was replaced by an atmosphere of dejection. Inquisitive eyes converged upon Dr. Athenaion. She could not resist a feeling to comment on Stanley's brief announcement."

"The college has been suffering from a steep budget deficit for more than five years. The Board of Trustees has recommended that some departments be closed. Philosophy was one of them. The faculty stood firmly against this recommendation, but their efforts were useless. The philosophy program was the primary victim. Unfortunately, non-profession-oriented programs were the first to go. Philosophy is a human vocation, not a profession. The majority of the Board members think that the philosophy program can and should be suspended until the college recovers its financial health."

"And now?" Dora asked.

"I shall try to search for a teaching position at another college. All shall be well, Mother." Dora did not respond to her daughter but sank into a lake of solemn silence.

"Anat is—" Stanley began to respond on behalf of his sister, but he could not because a loud knock at the front door reverberated loudly throughout the house. He left his sister's chair and rushed to the door. A firefighter met his eyes.

"Is Dr. Athenaion here?"

"She is urgently needed at her apartment. May I speak with her?"

"Of course!" Stanley said with quivering lips. He ran to the living room and returned with his sister.

"I am sorry to report, Dr. Athenaion, that your apartment is on fire—"

"On fire?"

"Yes, Dr. Athenaion. You should come with me as soon as possible."

"Can my brother and I drive her to the apartment?" Stanley asked.

"Certainly!" Stanley suggested Kenny because Kenny was a lawyer.

Dr. Athenaion and her brothers followed the firefighter to the apartment. It was already demolished. A few pillars and some fallen boards were still burning, but the whole frame, including the furniture, except some metallic objects such as the dishwasher and the washing machine, was reduced to ash mounds. Even the machines were half melted! Involuntarily, Dr. Athenaion rushed to what used to be her study. She examined the remains. The books, the notes, the computer—everything was gone! She stood next to the melted computer and what was her desk and dragged a long sad look over them. She touched the ashes, as well as the melted computer with her hand the way a mother touches her sick child and remained silent for several long seconds! Tears rolled over her cheeks. She wiped them stealthily and then joined her brothers.

"Everything," she murmured, "everything!"

"No, my dear Anat, you are here. Therefore, nothing is gone!" Stanley emphasized!

"No, Stanley. Those mounds and eddies of ash you see there," she said, pointing with her hand to the practically leveled library, "are parts of me." Stanley understood the importance of his sister's remark. He was about to console her but could not because the firefighter approached her.

"I am terribly sorry, Dr. Athenaion. We did our best to save your place. The building had already collapsed when we arrived at the scene. It must have been an unusually ferocious fire. I have never seen such a destructive fire in my life. The flames were eating up the wood with the speed of light. Confounding! The fire was so hot, we could barely come close to the building," he said and shook his head. "Even the kitchen machines melted. It was like the fire of hell was burning up this apartment. I really cannot understand it."

"Were you able to identify the cause?" Kenny asked.

"Not yet. We shall look for clues tomorrow. The only thing we can now do is file a report at the office."

"Fine!" Kenny said with a subdued voice.

The firefighters who battled the fire were waiting for Dr. Athenaion and her brothers at the Fire Department. Gloom emanated from their faces. "That fire was a doozy!" One of the firefighters standing at the counter said."

It was impossible to rescue any of your belongings, not even the metallic objects. It seemed as if the gods of the underground were pouring out their wrath on your house. But I think the insurance company should compensate you for everything."

"Everything?" Dr. Athenaion asked with a slight tinge of sadness in her voice.

"Yes, everything. We shall emphasize that the fire demolished the building and every object in it. You can be sure they will pay for everything! We shall send a copy of the report to the insurance company tomorrow."

"Thank you!" Kenny said when he received the report from the chief officer. "We really appreciate your help!"

The Athenaion family did not have a conversation, or anything close to it, that evening. They were reflecting, stipulating, and evaluating the calamities that befell their Anat, and they were thinking of ways to help her sail through that devastating storm. "Everything she had vanished into thin air by one stroke of bad luck," Antoinette marveled, "nothing is secure, and nothing lasts in this world!"

"Some things are secure, and some things last, Mother!" Maggie murmured. She looked at Kenny with sad eyes. She did not want anyone to hear her remarks. He grasped the meaning of her look but said nothing. He was unable to see, feel, or think about anything at that moment. Who in their wildest imagination could have thought that one of the most successful, respectable, and admirable women in Jackson would be jobless and homeless in one instant? Although this inconceivable fact forced itself into the minds of Dora's extended family, and although they were willing and ready to shoulder the burden those calamities inflicted upon her, Dr. Athenaion did not allow them to disturb her peace of mind. She felt the vibes of their sadness and their compassion. But for some strange reason, she was unable to accept anyone's help, not out of selfishness or stinginess but out of a deep feeling of love. When you love someone, she believed, you do not wish them to suffer emotionally, intellectually, or materially. Your innermost desire is to promote their sense of wellbeing, to protect them against any possible harm, even when you are suffering intense pain. But more importantly, Dr. Athenaion believed that neither she nor anyone else could have influenced the course of the events that led to those calamities. *They did take place, and they are now in the belly of the past.* No one could do anything about them. Getting angry or rebellious about them, or indulging in self-pity because of them, would not only be a sign of weakness, it would also be useless.

The rational thing to do was to maintain a semblance of inner calm, of self-composure, and design a sensible plan of action. This is the sort of attitude Dr. Athenaion assumed when she faced those gloomy faces. With a soft, compassionate smile hovering over her lips, she surveyed those faces, for she could not focus on them simultaneously, and said, "This is not the end of the world; this is the beginning of the world. Do not feel sorry for me, please. Losing my job and apartment is not as catastrophic you seem to think. Losing one's mind, one's freedom, one's moral integrity is the real catastrophe of human life. I shall find another job and another apartment. I beg you to look forward, not backward. We are born to look forward, not backward! The land of the future is the land of our life. The land of the past is the land of death. We should dwell in the land of life, not in the land of death! I shall always treasure the rays of sadness that flow from your hearts into mine. I am reluctant to feel the sadness, and I do not wish to feel it, I feel the love that gave rise to those rays. This love converts sadness into a feeling of inner contentment." Dr. Athenaion stopped, walked to the wine cabinet, and fetched two bottles from it. She asked Kenny to open them and Felicity to distribute wine glasses to the family. "If the power of love could transmute water into wine," she added, "then it can transmute the feeling of sadness into a feeling of joy, the feeling of frustration into a feeling of gratification, and the feeling of loneliness into a feeling of fellowship."

"It is good to drink a cup of pleasure now and then, but it is better to drink a cup of joy as frequently as we can. The delight of the first recedes as soon as we empty the cup, the delight of the second remains a flame of life in our minds. The first keeps us tethered to the earth, the second transports us to heaven. Love is the sole foundation in our lives." Dr. Athenaion raised her glass a little and added, "I propose a toast to your presence in my life, to the love this presence signifies! Please, smile before you leave this home! This is my strongest desire!" She took a sip of wine and sat next to her mother. She held her mother's hand and squeezed it. "You are going to have a guest tonight, Mother," she whispered.

"This is your home. Your room is still as you left it." Dora also returned in a whisper.

Shortly after Dr. Athenaion thanked her family with a toast, exactly the way her father would have done, Brenda and her mother declared their intention to leave. "I tried to smile, my dear," Antoinette said to Dr. Athenaion when she was saying good-bye to her, "but honestly, I could not. I stand in awe before you. This is the only feeling I could muster. It is a feeling of respect, admiration, and profound love. You are not one of the most eminent teachers in Jackson by accident. The magic of your humanity, of your honesty, of your understanding, is overwhelming." Antoinette bent over Dr. Athenaion and kissed her on the head. She left the family in silence. Brenda kissed Dr. Athenaion on the cheek and followed her mother. The other members of the family did the same. "No Athenaion can feel lonely in this family," David said and hugged her warmly. Stanley, Kenny, and Maggie remained a little longer. "I shall fetch a copy of the Fire Department report tomorrow and take it to the insurance company. There is no need for you to worry about this errand. Maggie will be here tomorrow afternoon. She and Brenda will assist you in doing some shopping at Macrae's."

"I can do it alone."

"Yes, but there is no reason for you to be alone. It is better to be together than alone!" Dr. Athenaion moved closer to Kenny and Maggie and hugged them.

"And me?" Stanley said teasingly. "Do I need to do something to deserve a hug from those warm arms? How about a short visit to the computer shop—of course when you have a free minute?"

"Oh, Stanley! Don't push me down any further! I am already drowned in a sea of kindness!"

"I shall bring you my back-up computer tomorrow. We can go to Best Buy. The geeks there will install a program for you. It should be ready within two to three days."

"But—"

"No buts! All of us should be grateful to you for allowing us to grow in the power of giving, my dear!"

Mowt was sitting in Dr. Athenaion's swivel chair when she opened the door of her office the next morning. She froze at the threshold, her eyes impaling him! A burst of confusion intermixed with anger swept through her mind. The mere sight of his face conjured up the image of her demolished apartment. This image was succeeded by the image of the termination of her position as a full-time faculty member at Union. She trembled! She could neither belittle nor ignore Mowt's existence any longer. He was, in some mysterious way, a way she could not comprehend, real. He was destructive, and she should take his threats seriously—but how? How can you fight a delusive, perhaps imaginary entity, an entity that calls itself the God of Death? How can you stand in a duel with an entity that asks you to abnegate your very self, your identity, the being you are? How can you accept to lose your humanity and reduce yourself to a lump of flesh? Alas, who will believe you if you reveal the truth of your encounter with such an entity? What if Dr. Athenaion informed her family that the two calamities that befell her a few days ago were wrought by the God of Death, wouldn't they mock her and treat her as a mentally disturbed woman? Those calamities are universal; they happen to people frequently. They can be explained logically, even scientifically! And yet, what seemed until then unbelievable to Dr. Athenaion, is now becoming believable but in a weird, absurd way. She couldn't doubt the existence of that apparition, which was no apparition, sitting at her swivel chair.

"Welcome to your office, Dr. Athenaion!" he said and sat in the chair opposite hers. "Please sit down! Your chair is waiting for you, so am I!"

"I am not, and it is not a good morning! Leave this office immediately!"

"You are not in a position to dismiss me."

"I am!"

"You are a defiant woman!"

"You are not worth defying! Just vanish."

"I am glad to see that you now recognize *who* I am. You are making progress."

"You are a silly delusion, a silly intrusion."

"Am I? If I were you, you too would be a silly existence. Are you?"

"Stop this nonsense!"

"I cannot until you stop yours. You see, instead of heeding my advice, you trampled on it. That was a huge mistake. The torch your father handed to your mother is now moving to your hand. You are becoming a high priest of humanity. Do you think I shall allow you to build a temple of humanity? Your family is slowly becoming an oasis of love. Very soon, it will be a kingdom. Oh, no, I cannot allow this to happen."

"You cannot stop—"

"I can, and I will. Was the closing of the philosophy department at Union an accident? I had to eliminate the whole department primarily to undercut any possible relationship you might establish with the college. Again, was the fire that demolished your apartment an accident? Even the firefighter asserted more than once that he had never seen such a ferocious fire, such a destructive fire in his life. Do you think that I am a delusion? Do you still think that I am a god of words and not a god of action? Those ordinary events are no more than samples of what I can and will do if you do not desist from working on your human community project. You are witnessing a god of action, Dr. Athenaion!"

"You can destroy everything I have, even my body, but you cannot destroy my will, my resolve to pursue, and hopefully to implement my project. I do not stand on your ground, I stand on the ground of humanity, where the human spirit has been weaving its way to higher levels of being through the course of cosmic history. This ground is the ground of love. Neither you nor anyone of your agents can come close to it. The courage of those who stand on this ground surpasses your capacity of understanding."

"You are insulting me."

"You are incapable of insult! How can an entity deprived of human feeling be insulted?"

"Your insult is an expression of contempt."

"But, you are contemptible."

"In your eyes, only in your eyes!"

"Do you have eyes?"

"I do what my uncle the Devil asks me to do. He is a greater god."

"Therefore, you have no eyes."

"I see you."

"Do you?'

"I see the woman with whom I am now speaking."

"*Do you see me*?"

"You must be a sophist."

"Then you have no knowledge of philosophy and philosophers."

"You must desist from your work on the human community project," Mowt said, suddenly changing the subject of the conversation.

"I shall not."

"Are you willing to accept the consequences of your decision?"

"Yes."

"Are you sure?"

"Yes!" Dr. Athenaion said with a sarcastic smirk on her lips.

"You shall regret your insolence," Mowt said, and then with angry eyes added before disappearing, "we shall soon meet again."

Although she felt justified in resisting Mowt's threats and was willing to continue her duel with him, Dr. Athenaion could not prevent several questions and doubts from coursing through her mind as she sat in her chair after his disappearance. What if he succeeded in obstructing her work? If he could, how? He said he would not cause her death, for this was the Devil's task, could he inflict harm on her mind or will? So far, her encounter with him had been a secret—how long could she keep this affair a secret? But could she? Even though it seemed that Mowt was keeping his promises, because he had kept all the promises he made, was he real after all? But again, was her line of reasoning delusive?

These questions did not deter Dr. Athenaion from emptying the drawers of her desk. Julie was already packing the books in the boxes when she returned from her one o'clock lecture. "You cannot leave the college, Dr. Athenaion," she said with tears in her eyes, "the students love you; they will miss you sorely. Union College will be a worse place after you leave." Her tears fell on the books she was packing. Dr. Athenaion walked to her assistant and hugged her.

"My departure is essential for the survival of the college. This is more important than my tenure." She could not add one word to this response primarily because a feeling of guilt, of moral anxiety, suddenly crept into her consciousness. Was she responsible for the financial crisis of the college? And her apartment—was she responsible for its demolition? What if this monstrous entity, perhaps apparition, is real? Can she morally justify this and perhaps the other destructive events Mowt might inflict directly or indirectly upon her or her family? When you find yourself between the cruel tongs of guilt and doubt, you feel like you are about to suffocate. This is how Dr. Athenaion felt when she held Julie within her arms. She wept, and she could not stop the tears from falling on her assistant's head. "Let us call it a day, Julie! We can resume the packing tomorrow," she murmured in a sad voice.

"But—" Julie tried to respond to her teacher and mentor, but she could not because a flood of emotions checked that response.

"Tomorrow!" Dr. Athenaion repeated. "There is a tomorrow every day, my dear!"

"There will be a tomorrow when we wake up, but it will never be the same—not for me and not for the college."

"No one knows. It may be better for you and for the college after I leave."

"Never!" Julie said and began packing her bag. The teacher watched her silently for a few seconds with melancholy eyes and then slowly returned to her chair. But she did not remain there for long. She had a few errands to run. Her old room was practically vacant and needed a few objects. Ironically, she did not go home that afternoon.

Christine Metcalf, Kenny's secretary, knocked lightly at the door of his room, but he did not respond to her knock. She knocked again, this time more loudly, still he did not respond. She waited a few seconds and knocked one more time. He did not answer. She was concerned. Although against his wishes, she knocked one more time and opened the door. Kenny was on the phone. He looked at her with an obvious expression of displeasure. She ignored his reaction, placed a note at his desk, and pointed with her finger to the note. "Read it immediately," she whispered. With the telephone receiver still attached to his ear, he read it. He abruptly said to the person on the other side of the line, "I shall call you back!" Without even looking at Christine, he hurried to the police department. He introduced himself to the attending officer as Dr. Athenaion's attorney and requested an audience with her.

"You must be her brother," the office said, "Dr. Athenaion is waiting for you. I am sorry, we never expected a person like her to be in this place, not Dr. Athenaion. My nephew took two courses with her. He adores her. Everyone who studies with her adores her. They sing her praises every time her name is mentioned. She should not be in this or any other jail. I am convinced that there is something wrong somewhere. Believe me, if I tell you that if it were up to me, I would not even think of apprehending her. We simply have rules, and we have to follow them."

"I understand. Thank you!"

The officer led Kenny to Dr. Athenaion's cell. She was sitting on a wooden chair, almost in a fetal position, when the officer opened the door. Her elbows were resting on her knees, and her head was resting on her hands. Kenny ran to her and embraced her firmly. "What happened?" He asked after he freed her from his arms.

"I did some shopping at Macrae's a little while ago. When I approached my car in the parking lot and pulled out the keys from my briefcase, two men jumped me. They must have been lying in wait for me behind the car next to mine. We had a fight. The first thing they did was to yank the briefcase off my shoulder. I tried to prevent them from taking it, but they overpowered me and ran away with it. A man and a woman, who must be husband and wife, witnessed the incident. They sped toward me and asked if I were all right. I assured them that I was not harmed but that the men stole my briefcase. They informed me that they had called the police and that two officers were on their way to the Macrae's parking lot. They stayed with me until the police car entered the parking lot. Before they left, they gave me their names and address and assured me that they were willing to be witnesses in court if witnesses were needed. The man remarked that the police department had a list of muggers in Jackson. "They know how to find them. They will arrest them rather fast," he said.

"The policemen escorted me to the department primarily to file a report about the incident. But, to my surprise, and I should say to my shock, I was told that I was under arrest. "'Why?" I asked.

"'Drug charges,' the officer said.

"'There must be a mistake, Officer!'

"'No, Dr. Athenaion," he replied. "We have just apprehended the muggers. They are in jail. They returned your briefcase. We inspected it to ascertain your identity. We discovered in it one pound of cocaine and three ounces of heroin.'

"'Impossible! I do not use drugs, and I am strongly opposed to them.'

"'We cannot make decisions here. The court makes such decisions,' the officer said.

"'And now?'

"'You have to stay here in jail until—'

"'Can I speak with a lawyer,' I asked, interrupting him.

"'Of course, you can!'"

"Here I am, Kenny. This is all I know."

"I am afraid you shall have to spend the night here. But I shall furnish bail on you as soon as possible. You should be released from this place tomorrow around noon. We have no choice in the matter. Please, be patient. I am terribly sorry about this. You have had more than your fair share of unhappy incidents!" He stopped for a moment, hesitated a little, and then continued, "What has been happening to you boggles my mind—any sane mind!" Kenny said with a deep sigh, one that expressed a deep feeling of dejection.

"It is you who should be patient, dear Kenny! I shall be fine. With tears in his eyes, Kenny embraced his sister for a long time and left her without looking at her. He could not. He was stuck in a thick puddle of sadness.

But the reverberations of these unhappy incidents were not restricted to the walls of the jail, or to those of the police department. They found their way into the Athenaion family, the Union College campus, and the whole Jackson area. On the following morning, the Clarion Ledger carried the following headline in bold letters: The Eminent Dr. Anat Athenaion of Union College in Jail on Drug Charges. The article that recounted her arrest and spotlighted the fact that one pound of cocaine and three ounces of heroin were found in her briefcase and that she was in a brawl with two muggers who were apprehended on drug dealing charges a few years ago.

The celebrated Dr. Athenaion in a brawl with two criminals over a large bag of cocaine? This was the juicy news of the day in Jackson, Mississippi, and in fact, it was the juiciest news in more than a month. Dora's phone began to ring in the late morning that day and did not stop until late afternoon when she sadly disconnected it. Her biological and adopted families converged upon her house that evening. They were anxious about Anat. They could not believe the story of the Clarion Ledger. They simply could not believe such stories about the most virtuous, most upright, most accomplished woman they had ever met. They were convinced that a jealous teacher, colleague, or lover must have concocted this whole incident simply to harm her! They were ready to help their sister in every possible way. "What do you think, Kenny?" Dora asked after the family had gathered in the living room that evening.

"I think it is a setup. I shall discuss it with my colleagues, and maybe with Judge Ethridge if I have to. I trust his advice. I am sure that no one will believe that my sister is a drug dealer or user." He paused for a second, cast an abstract look at his mother, and added, "I do not understand why the Clarion Ledger did not explain or question the nature of the brawl and the true identity of the muggers. They should have interviewed my sister before they printed the article. This is irresponsible journalism. Many naïve people, especially those who do not know my sister well, will be inclined to believe that she is a drug dealer or user, or both. However, what concerns me is not only the psychological and professional harm done to her but why and who is trying to harm my sister."

"I agree with you about the Clarion Ledger," Charlotte interjected, "I really think they were looking for a hot news item. But how do you confront the main newspaper in Jackson? Do you know that many people believe the Clarion Ledger naively and uncritically as if what they read in it is the truth and nothing but the truth?"

"Should we listen or even take into serious consideration public opinion, especially when it is shallow or biased?"

"I really think that we should not over-react," Stanley suggested, "too much harm has already been done; we cannot do anything about it. Therefore, it is prudent to be patient and wait until Kenny consults with the members of his firm and perhaps Judge Ethridge. The facts will surface sooner or later. I make this remark with a heavy heart, a heart that bleeds for my sister. How can a woman like Anat spend a night, or even a second, in jail? The only jail she can be in is Heaven!"

But Dr. Athenaion was spending the night in jail, in the jail of Jackson, Mississippi. She was not confronting the Clarion Ledger, public opinion, or the Union College community, she was confronting the *source* of the calamities that were befalling her, Union College, and even the Clarion Ledger! Frankly, she was indifferent to public opinion, the opinion of the Union community, or to what the Clarion Ledger wrote or might write! Her primary concern was the safety and wellbeing of her family and the continued prosperity of the college. She knew that her destiny was intertwined with that of the college. Isn't the quest for truth, justice, freedom, and progress the reason for being of the college, as well as her own being?

This train of thought, which was fluttering in her mind as she reclined on the cot in her cell, was interrupted by the sudden appearance of Mowt. "I keep my promises," he said."

"I am not interested in your promises!"

"But you are, and you must be interested in them. Drug dealers and users are apprehended every day. Nobody pays attention to them, and no newspaper writes front-page articles about them. But when the eminent Dr. Athenaion is thrown in jail for drug dealing and using, the situation is different. The fall of virtue, of human excellence, from the top of the high mountain of excellence into the valley of mediocrity creates a big bang—don't you think?" Mowt said with an unmistakable tone of sarcasm in his voice. "How does it feel to be in this dungeon-like cell? How does it feel to be treated like a drug dealer and user, as a criminal? How does it feel to be stripped of that halo of eminence, of majesty, and stand naked before yourself and the world? How does it feel to be bathed in disgrace? Tell me, please!" Mowt grinned sarcastically and added, "Are you really the genuine philosopher, citizen, and Dr. Athenaion everyone thinks you are or are you simply a fraud? Don't you really wish to keep that image of respectability? Who in their right mind would wish to lose it?" Mowt stopped again, but this time he showed the ugly side of his face and the more hideous form of his teeth and disdainfully continued, "Oh, Dr. Athenaion, you know that you are the subject of gossip, the kind that spreads goosebumps throughout the body and soul. Do you know that the Jackson community are savoring the titillations of your delicious news? Do you know that many of the Union professors, those who suppressed their envy and jealousy of you for a long time, are now delighting in your imprisonment? If only you could see yourself in the mirror of truth! Try to look into it. Your eyes are keen, very keen—you cannot miss it! If you do, you will, without a shred of doubt, see a ridiculous, pathetic, and despicable image of yourself. Yes, Dr. Athenaion, that is the image you will see!"

"How I look and feel is not any of your business. Leave immediately! How many times have I asked you to stay away from me? Speaking with you is the worst kind of punishment a human being can tolerate! Just leave my presence!"

"But your presence is my business, my very business, my only business in Jackson at present. I shall not leave it until you consent to abandon your work on the human community project." Dr. Athenaion cast a scornful glance at the intruder and said:

"You can strip me of my reputation, my job, my possessions, even my family, but you cannot strip me of my will, and you cannot shake my faith in the sacredness of humanity. I am my will, and I am the spark of humanity whose vision devastates the foundation of your being. You have no authority over me! You can take away my computer, my papers, my pens, and my ink, but you cannot take away my mind because I shall write my project with the hand, paper, pen, and ink of my mind. Neither you nor anyone of your minions can prevent me from pursuing the dream of my life."

"You really are an obstinate woman."

"It seems that you have installed yourself as the ultimate standard of wisdom—of knowledge, truth, and goodness."

"I have my powers, and I have my charge. Death is my domain, and I am king in my domain. I shall do whatever is in my power to make sure that your project never sees the light of day!"

"Try me!

"How can you defy me when you are so humiliated when you are thrown in jail like a cheap criminal?"

"My eyes do not see the wretchedness of this cell or any ugliness you may inflict upon me, and they are indifferent to public opinion. Has it occurred to you that public opinion exists in the mind of the public, and your hate exists in your mind, and nowhere else? Neither your hate nor public opinion will leap from your mind or the mind of the public and influence me. They mean nothing to me! And has it occurred to you that he who hates suffers from their own hate! All your physical and social torture shall remain under my control. Apparently, you neither see nor understand the power of the human will, the will that is founded in truth and goodness. My eyes shall see nothing but truth and goodness, and they will stay in their light, not in your darkness!"

"You are defiant!" Mowt said, venomous rays of hate flowing from his eyes. "I shall give you one more chance to reconsider my request."

"Begone!"

A thick cloud of gloom settled in the Athenaion home and the Jackson City jail that night. Although Dr. Athenaion was steadfast in her defiance of Mowt, although she would be released from her cell the following afternoon, and although she strongly felt that she was justified in her defiance and that she was willing to die rather than surrender her will to a dubious, diabolical, and destructive entity, she hardly slept that night. The source of her anxiety was neither fear nor doubt, but concern for her family and Union College. What right did Mowt have, regardless of whether he was the God of Death, to cause harm to innocent people? Wasn't she, in the final analysis, the real cause of all that confusion and destruction wreaked in her life and the life of her family? But what if she complied with Mowt's request, wouldn't she be the cause of greater harm in the near or distant future? On the other hand, regardless of whether harm or wellbeing would be promoted, was she justified in making a decision of such gravity? *Was she her sister's keeper*?

Moreover, Mowt promised to inflict more harm upon her—what kind of harm was he planning? Will it involve her family or other people? Prevention of harm and promotion of good were sacrosanct principles to Dr. Athenaion. For her, they were not written by human beings but were created in Heaven by the hand of God. How could she apply these two principles wisely? It is not enough to believe in truth; it is equally important to act on it wisely! These and a host of other ideas crowded her mind during the early hours of the night. She succumbed to sleep a little later only because fatigue overpowered her consciousness.

The jailer woke Dr. Athenaion at eight o'clock in the morning. He brought her a small breakfast, but she declined it. She did not feel a need for food. The only need that dominated her mind was the need to dismiss Mowt from her life. Fortunately, the jailer returned to her cell in midmorning and led her to the reception room. Kenny was waiting for her. He had already submitted the bail documents to the attending officer. "I am really sorry for this tangle, Dr. Athenaion. I know you will be completely exonerated. My family was shocked when they heard what happened to you. Don't leave her, Mr. Athenaion!" The officer implored compassionately.

"Thank you most kindly, sir!"

CHAPTER SEVEN

The Final Battle Between Dr. Athenaion and the God of Death

As they did the previous evening, the Athenaion family gathered at Dora's home. They ate an informal supper and discussed the grueling experiences of Dr. Athenaion. They voiced unqualified solidarity with her. Except for a few specific questions related to the way the muggers jumped her and how she protected herself from their brutal assault, Dr. Athenaion listened to their remarks and opinions in silence, but pensively. She was grateful for their love and support, but she also felt that her problems should not encumber their lives. Mowt's image hovered in the living room a few times. His warning, "I shall see you sooner than you think!" rang in her ears several times.

"What does he have in store for me?" This question pressed itself sharply upon her mind and left in it a feeling of fearful expectation. The threat implicit in it should be intimidating, if not fearful, but she remained calm. Her commitment to her life project was as firm as an unmoving mountain made of granite. The only response to this threat was simply, "Let it be!" She was willing to assume responsibility for her decision and, more importantly, for the kind of human being she was. But then, why burden this generous and loving family? What is their mistake? Why should they suffer with her? What kind of wrong did she do to deserve this unfolding stream of calamities? But, furthermore, what is her mistake? Alas, should we not *give and receive love and be loved gracefully*? What magnified the intensity of her inner struggle was the fact that she could not reveal the secret cause, the diabolical cause, of this whole unfolding tragedy. And yet, she decided to plow her way through this developing catastrophe with all the courage and wisdom she could summon from her heart and mind.

The following morning, Dr. Athenaion went to her office, as she always did. She had one more lecture to give, but it was her last lecture at the college. She intended to deliver it the way she delivered every other lecture, without regard to how the students might receive her or react to the scandal that was hanging in the dark sky of her life. She was always indifferent to public opinion—why should she pay any attention to it now? The only voice she heeded was the voice of her moral sense and the sense of wisdom. Normally, if you are guilty, cracks will appear in your behavior of character sooner or later. But she was not guilty, therefore, why should she be concerned about a possible adverse or strange reaction from her students?

Sadly, her students did not welcome her as they always did. On the contrary, many of them were absent, and those who were present did not seem to pay serious attention to her presence in the lecture room. She understood the meaning of this radical change in attitude, as well as its cause. Nevertheless, this change did not influence her. She began her lecture with her usual thoughtful and enthusiastic presentation of the main questions she was planning to discuss. But something unexpected, something extraordinary happened in the middle of the lecture. Dr. Athenaion suddenly stopped. Her lips quivered violently, her eyes fluttered, she lost her balance and then collapsed on the floor. She fainted. Hums and hisses resounded throughout the lecture room. Some students called security, while others called an ambulance.

Within a few minutes, Dr. Athenaion was in the Emergency Room of St. Dominic's hospital. The attending doctor, who was still a resident and must have taken a course with Dr. Athenaion, immediately called his former teacher, Dr. Stanley Athenaion. The resident and two other doctors were able to recover Dr. Athenaion's consciousness. A few minutes later, Stanley arrived at the Emergency Room. He read his sister's medical chart. The first thing he did was a variety of blood tests and a comprehensive CT scan with a special focus on the brain. Unfortunately, a large tumor was discovered, and a biopsy was performed to determine whether it was malignant, but the results had to wait until the following day.

Stanley recommended that his sister spend the night at the hospital. He called Kenny and informed him of his sister's accident. Kenny had just returned from an interview with the muggers before they were moved to the penitentiary. "I shall be there shortly," he said, and in fact, he joined his brother and sister in less than fifteen minutes. He hugged Anat and kissed her on the forehead three times. He left many tears on her head. He could not speak. His lips were frozen. He hugged her again while trying to speak, but still failed. He looked at Stanley with painfully sad, troubled eyes. Stanley, too could not speak. He summoned a smile that was tender and compassionate. "We need to inform Mother of what had happened," Stanley murmured. Then, turning his face toward his sister, he added, Mother needs to know, so does the family. You shall spend the night here, my dear. We do not need another mishap if, for some reason, you have another fainting spell. Your room will be ready shortly. It is not wise to do this on the phone. Kenny and I should relay the news in person. Anyway, the family will be with you as soon as they hear the news. They will be severely disappointed if they do not know about it sooner rather than later." The two brothers accompanied their sister to her room. They kissed her on the head and left with heavy hearts.

But Dr. Athenaion was not left alone in her room. Mowt paid her another visit as soon as her brothers had gone. He sat at the foot of her bed. "How is the daughter of love doing?" He asked mockingly.

"How I am doing is not your concern. Leave!"

"Did someone tell you that you are a mush?"

"Does the mere mention of love disconcert you? Does the power of reason unsettle you?"

"Those two forces, love, and reason, are disgusting. They secrete the nastiest juices into my stomach!"

"Why?"

"They are my worst enemies. I was created to hate them and subvert them."

"Why?"

"They are sparks of the creative power of the God of Love."

"Is it because they are the source of humanity? Is it because they are the highest emanation of The Creator?"

"You are speaking cryptically."

"Well, then, let me decipher my cryptogram. Humanity is absolutely valuable because it is capable of freedom, of self-determination. It can exist in the world as a free agent, that is, because it can design and realize its life, because it is capable of self-creation. Only God, the supreme being that created the universe, is distinguished, among an infinite number of aspects, by this dimension. Was it an accident that some religions hold that human beings were created in the image of God?"

"In the image of God?"

"Yes."

"You are not in the habit of contradicting yourself."

"How did I contradict myself?"

"If God is an infinity of dimensions, how can this minuscule human being be created in the image of such an infinite being?"

"First, if infinity is an essential aspect of God, then every aspect of his being should reflect his infinity. Next, reason and love are crucial dimensions of his infinite being. These are powers, and they are infinite in their capacity of loving and knowing, even though they are finite, in the sense that they exist in a finite being like a human person. Human beings are created in the image of God in so far as they are able to actualize the powers of love and reason. How can one commit self-contradiction when they make this kind of claim? Everything people attribute to God is based on their knowledge of this dimension. But although it is one dimension, it is infinitely rich in its being. And yet, this dimension reveals much, amazingly much, about the kind of being God is. If I were you, Mowt, I would not be foolishly arrogant in my claims and pretensions. You are no more than a negligible particle of being if such a particle exists."

"However, what matters is not this cosmological technicality but the fact, which you should always remember, that not all human beings can be bought and sold. Only those who are deprived of the opportunity to grow in their humanity, those who necessarily live in your cave of darkness, those who do not comprehend the significance of love and reason, those who do not live in and by their light, yes, those and only those may crumble under your pressure or may be seduced by the pleasures and glories you promise them. Has it occurred to you that a being who is capable of self-creation will defend their intellectual, moral, and physical integrity to the death?"

"Are you sure?"

"I cannot be absolutely sure only because I did not have this kind of experience before, but I am sure that I am willing to defy the God of Death no matter the severity of the pain he might inflict upon me."

"You are not as strong as you think you are!" Mowt said scornfully.

"I never said I was strong, and I never thought of myself as a strong person. I am what I am, and I shall always act according to the powers that make me who and what I am. I refuse to be treated as a commodity."

"Can I infer from what you have said that you will not desist from your work on the human community project?"

"You certainly can! You have my answer; it was, it is, and it will always be the same, no! Frankly, you have been consuming my time and patience. Don't overstep the boundaries of appropriateness. I cannot tolerate your nonsense anymore. Leave my room now!"

"First, you cannot make me leave. Second, you should know what to expect in your life and the life of your family if you do not comply with my request. Don't you think that your family is already agonizing over your plights? I have not yet begun!"

"Threatening me again?"

"When conversation—"

"What!" Dr. Athenaion exclaimed, unable to control her frustration with Mowt, "Physical and psychological injury? Death? Harming innocent people?"

"I do not threaten. I act! When the method of conversation fails, I try the method of intimidation—"

"You must be a small-minded god," Dr. Athenaion said, interrupting Mowt. "Not even a child would resort to such a method to rob me of my freedom, of my dignity!"

"Don't worry! I shall not inflict physical harm on your family, although I shall try to squeeze the last drop of physical life from you if I can only to make you comply with my request. I am the son of evil, and I shall employ all the evil methods of treatment at my disposal. I aim at the human will, and your will is my target!"

"What course of action do you plan for me, then?" Mowt grinned disdainfully.

"I shall undermine your project."

"You cannot, and you will not! You do not even exist!"

"How can you doubt my existence if you are conversing with me?

"I am not conversing with you. You are incapable of conversation. You are dueling with me. The sophists were more proficient than you in spuriously using logic to their advantage." Dr. Athenaion paused for a second and said rather impatiently, "Stop your drivel and leave!"

"I do not leave, I vanish when I decide. But before I vanish, let me remind you that I am a god of action, not of words and not merely of threats." Dr. Athenaion did not respond to his reminder. Her silence fell upon Mowt like an avalanche of solid rocks!

"This is my last warning!" Mowt added. Dr. Athenaion remained silent. "You will regret your stubbornness!" He said and vanished.

Although Dr. Athenaion stood her ground in her conversation with Mowt, and although she remained firm in her refusal to cooperate with him, she could not stop Master Doubt from crawling into her consciousness. He wore a solemn but compassionate expression. His eyes, which seemed like the eyes of an eagle, thrust a sharp look into Dr. Athenaion's eyes: "What if Mowt is real, what if he is really the God of Death, and what if he is serious in his claim that he would undermine your project? He reasoned rather well when he argued that if he were not real, you would not be willing to converse with him, but you did. Otherwise, you would be hallucinating; therefore, he must be real. And if he is real, don't you think you should be taking him seriously?"

"But how can he appear and disappear at will?"

"I know you have critically analyzed and evaluated this line of reasoning immediately following his first visit to you, and I know that you are reluctant to discuss this whole episode of your life with any of your family, friends, or colleagues, because no one would believe your narrative. On the contrary, they'll deliver you to a mental institution or recommend that you see a psychiatrist, not to mention the fact that you would be dismissed from Union and ridiculed by everyone around you. Your reluctance to discuss it even with your sister or brothers is wise, but this would not diminish the gravity of the situation you are in. What if Mowt inflicts physical or mental harm upon you? What if he disrupts the course of your life and devastates it—are you prepared for this possibility? Notice: I am not asking, or even implying, that you do as Mowt asks. But it is prudent to be prepared for the worst," Master Doubt stopped, looked at her reflectively, and added, "and for the best!"

"The best?"

"Yes."

"What do you mean?"

"Suppose he is real and succeeds in undermining your project—you lose. But suppose he is real but fails to undermine your project—you win, and then you emerge from this battle with Mowt as a stronger person, and *you emerge as a stronger force of good in a society that is in urgent need of goodness*!"

"What intrigues me is not merely the intrusion of such a repugnant entity into my life, if he is a real, but whether such an entity is at all possible in our world."

"Why not? Well, you speak of being and non-being. Have you experienced non-being somewhere or in some way?"

"No."

"But you say it must exist, for otherwise, we cannot speak of being. How can you explain change if you do not assume the existence of non-being? Things perish—into what do they perish if non-being does not exist? I do not aim, in these remarks, to convince you that a God of Death exists, I only wish that you entertain the possibility that what we consider as real, at the human or natural level, may not be the only types or sense of 'real.' As you argued cogently moments ago, the creator of the universe reveals only one dimension of his infinite being to us. Accordingly, it would be reasonable to say that if such a creator exists, and he does, then we should not rule out the possibility that other types of beings, quite different from ours, exist as well."

"Does this entail the possibility of a destructive, obnoxious reality such as Mowt?"

"What may seem evil to us may not be evil to the Creator. Even the events and the things we now judge as bad, frequently prove to be good. Human beings are not the final or most reliable judges of good and bad, right and wrong, or beauty and ugliness. Let me remind you of my own theory of cosmic creation. If this creation is an on-going process, and it is, we should grant that it is an on-going g process of perfection, of becoming more perfect than it is at any present moment. This implies that it aims at perfection. But if it is in the process of being perfected, then it necessarily contains imperfection. This imperfection, in the sphere of human and natural existence, is what we usually call evil. However, we cannot say that the process of cosmic creation does not contain imperfection. Let me illustrate this point with an analogy. The sculptor does not create the statute in one hewing of the slab of marble they are working with but shapes it according to the artistic vision in their imagination. The process of shaping the marble according to the vision, which is no more than a general schema, is indeterminate and unpredictable. Even the vision is constantly modified during the process of shaping the statue. Sometimes it undergoes a radical change by the time the process is completed because what exists in the imagination is, to a large extent, different from what exists in the marble. What exists in the imagination is mental, while the statue is physical. These two modes of existence are essentially incomparable. What exists in the imagination is a general possibility. The activity of transforming the marble into a statue frequently involves trial and error. How many a sculptor, and in general how many an artist, agonizes over the creation of their works? Although the activity of cosmic creation is generically different from the activity of artistic creation, and although it resists anthropomorphic characterization, can you imagine how much more agonizing, more arduous, and more challenging it is than the activity of artistic creation? Is there a justification for your reluctance to entertain the possibility of an entity like Mowt, even if its existence seems to contradict the laws of nature, as Mowt has argued? Let me remind you of a fact you know quite well, indeed much more than I, that formal logic is different from the logic of being. The cosmic process does not occur according to the rules of formal logic. I tend to think that the logic of philosophers is only one dimension of the logic that governs the cosmic process."

Master Doubt quietly crawled out Dr. Athenaion's consciousness, but she did not crawl into her bed quietly. On the contrary, she remained reclining in her bed for a long time battling a multitude of questions concerning the existence of Mowt—whether he was real and harmful, and if harmful, what kind of harm he might inflict upon her or her family. Master Doubt discussed an aspect of the problem she was facing but did not solve it. How could she solve it? It was her problem, not Master Doubt's. Master Doubt is an instigator of different ways of thinking and feeling, not of solving human problems. But, again, did Dr. Athenaion ask him or anyone for help? No, then why did he pay her that short visit? Was he a warm waft of reason, of love? Did she see herself in him? Maybe, maybe not. It may seem strange that our knowledge of the cosmos, of how it came into being, why it came into being, and who oversees its process is meager, very meager.

While Dr. Athenaion was struggling with the philosophical, moral, psychological, and material dynamics of the situation she was in, a completely different type of concern occupied the attention of the family soon after the arrival of the two brothers at their mother's home.

Well, Felicity was at home when Stanley and Kenny arrived from the hospital. Neither she nor her mother expected to see them together at this time of the week. The mere look at their sad faces aroused a frantic feeling of fear in their hearts. Felicity frowned: "What's wrong?" Dora, who was in the kitchen preparing supper for her and her daughter, left the kitchen when she heard the door of the house open and then close, and she also heard Felicity's frantic inquiry. She, too, was disturbed when she noticed the melancholy expressions of her two sons, and she too asked, "What is wrong, Stanley?"

"Anat is in the hospital!"

"In the hospital? Why?" Dora asked, a frightened expression on her face.

"She fainted in the middle of her last lecture at the college. She was immediately brought to St. Dominic's hospital. We did a multiplicity of tests. Unhappily, we discovered a tumor in the brain. We shall know whether it is malignant and if it is, whether it has spread tomorrow." Tears began to roll over Dora's and Felicity's cheeks when they heard this report. A swarm of "whys" gushed through Dora's mind: "She does not deserve all these blows, all these inflictions! Why God? Tell me! Tell me if you care, if you really care!"

"Any person would have lost faith in God if they were in her place." Dora sighed as she looked at her children abstractly without knowing what she was looking at, "Please, God, have mercy on her, if you are merciful," Dora said. Her faith in God, which was founded on the firmest rock you can imagine, began to break apart. She could not comprehend the meaning or reason for this barrage of inflictions. "This is not how good is rewarded; if it should be rewarded, this not how it should be rewarded. But if it should not be rewarded, then, why should we do good?" She said in a moment of hopeless desperation. She did not know whether she did or did not lose her faith in God! In fact, she did not care to know! Sadness intermixed with frustration can sometimes be debilitating.

"God does not interfere, at least not directly, in human lives," Kenny said, trying to pacify his mother.

"Somebody, some power, must be doing all this to her," Dora retorted.

"Wisdom underlies natural and human happenings, but it is not always obvious. I beg you to be patient, Mother. These events represent dark clouds. I am sure they will soon pass."

"Yes, they will soon pass," Stanley seconded his brother. "I think we need to inform the rest of the family of this new crisis!"

"I have already called Maggie and asked her to contact her sister and mother. They should be here any minute. We can visit Anat shortly after supper."

But another kind of conversation, one between Dr. Athenaion and the God of Death, was simultaneously taking place in Dr. Athenaion's room at the hospital.

"How does it feel to stand at the rim of all rims, at the rim that overlooks the infinite abyss? How does it feel to stand alone at the door of that infinite darkness, that is, in my kingdom?"

"Not again!" Dr. Athenaion said exasperated.

"You did not have to stand at that door, and, truthfully, you should not. You are still young and successful. You are beautiful. Why not let a good man delight in your beauty, and you delight in his delight? Why do you deny yourself the pleasures of this world? Try not to be foolish! I would fall in love with you instantly if I were not the God of Death."

"Stop this nonsense!" Dr. Athenaion snapped impatiently.

"I cannot. All you must do is simply consent to abandon your project on the development of a human community governed by technocrats! I am willing to give you one more chance, but not more than one, to change your mind. I would not be foolish if I were you. I promise you a socially respectable, an academically successful position, and a personally pleasant life. I also promise that you will be one of the most renowned philosophers in the world. Your office will be the Mecca of philosophy and philosophers. What do you think?"

"I shall not desist from my work on my project, no matter your fancy and seductive promises."

"What if the tumor on your brain suddenly grows out of proportion, and what if it is malignant?"

"Let it be!"

"Do you mean that you are willing to die a pathetic death, a pointless death, a cheap death, rather than desist from your work on your project?"

"First, it is not a silly project. It is a project of love. Everything in this world pales into insignificance in the presence of its light and, second, yes, I am willing to die rather than accept the glories you promised me. You can inflict any kind of pain on me, and you can strip me of everything I have; you can mutilate my body, and you can kill me if you feel a need to kill me, of course, out of spite and more realistically out of cowardice. Still, you cannot take away my humanity, because my humanity is a flame of love, of life! You are death. I am a lover; therefore, I am a flame of life. I do not derive my existence as a human being from you; I derive it from the God of Love."

"But I hate this god of yours."

"That is your problem, not mine. You can live in your hate, and certainly, you can sizzle in its flames forever."

"I am who I am."

"I, too, am who I am."

"I loathe you, Dr. Athenaion, and I shall forever loathe you. I shall dump tons of loathing in your life. I wish that you smell its nauseating odor every morning when you wake up and every evening when you go to bed. Even though it is hard to admit it, I cannot stand in the light of your love any longer." Mowt said and vanished, never to intrude into Dr. Athenaion's life again.

In fact, Dr. Athenaion felt in full possession of her physical, intellectual, and moral sensibilities the instant Mowt vanished. She called Stanley and Kenny and asked them to come to her room as soon as they could.

****

The spirit of evil that wreaked devastation in the life of Dr. Athenaion and her family vanished with the disappearance of Mowt. It was followed by a short period of reparation and gradual flourishing. The two muggers who assaulted her in Macrae's parking lot confessed, in their second interview at the police department, that they had placed the cocaine and heroin packages in her briefcase and that a drug dealer paid them a hefty sum of money to perform this criminal act. The following Sunday, the Clarion Ledger printed a short statement of apology on the front page. The editor confessed that the article he published a week earlier was a clear instance of incompetent journalism. The results of the biopsy were negative. The tumor was removed, and Dr. Athenaion could resume her normal daily activities without fear or hesitation. But the most important development, which reached the ears of the Union and the Jackson communities with a most pleasant bang, was a donation to Union College in the amount of one hundred million dollars by one of Dr. Athenaion's former students. He emphasized in his letter to the President of Union College that the money should be used to pay all the debt the college had incurred over the past five years, so that all the faculty who were dismissed from the college could be rehired, and that the Union Library could be named "The Dr. Anat Athenaion Library"!

As far as I know, Kenny and Maggie were married two months after their sister's recovery of her health and teaching position. Norman and Felicity were married three months after that. Stanley and Dr. Athenaion remained single. They decided to devote all their material and spiritual energies to the promotion of knowledge and social reform with Stanley focusing his attention on the artificial intelligence project and Dr. Athenaion on the human community project.

www.ingramcontent.com/pod-product-compliance
Lightning Source LLC
Chambersburg PA
CBHW070627310726
48982CB00001B/185

* 9 7 8 1 7 2 5 2 8 0 5 0 2 *